#24

MOTHER SETON
and The Sisters Of Charity

MOTHER SETON
and The Sisters Of Charity

by
Alma
Power-Waters

illustrated
by
John Lawn

VISION BOOKS

Farrar, Straus & Cudahy
Burns & Oates

New York
London

Nihil Obstat:
    Rt. Rev. Msgr. Peter B. O'Connor
        Censor Librorum

Imprimatur:
    ✠ Most Reverend Thomas A. Boland, S.T.D.
        Archbishop of Newark

Contents

Author's Note

Of the books which have been written about the beloved Elizabeth Seton, foundress of the Sisters of Charity in the United States, the author has found the following to be helpful: *Life of Mrs. Elizabeth A. Seton, the Foundress and First Superior of the Sisters or Daughters of Charity in the United States of America* by Charles I. White, *The Life Story of Mother Seton* by J. M. Loughborough, and *Mother Seton* by Rev. Joseph B. Code.

The History of the Catholic Church in the United States by John Dawson Gilmary Shea, *Memories of Many Years* by Robert Seton, and *Woman of Decision: The Life of Mother Mary Xavier Mehegan, Foundress of the Sisters of Charity of St. Elizabeth, Convent, New Jersey* by Sister Blanche Marie McEniry also contain interesting background material.

While the major incidents of Mother Seton's life here described are based on historical fact, it has been left to the author to reconstruct the setting and invent the dialog which will bring these scenes to life for young readers.

Personal thanks are due to the Sisters of Charity

who kindly supplied historical material and pictures, and to the following: Rt. Rev. Msgr. John S. Middleton, pastor, St. Peter's Church, New York City; Rev. George L. Hopkins, assistant pastor, Cathedral of the Assumption, Baltimore, Md.; Mr. Edward Morrison, Manuscript Division, New York Public Library; Miss Rita Keckeissen, librarian, St. Peter's Library, Barclay Street, New York City.

Chapter One

A SHIP COMES IN

ELIZABETH ANN BAYLEY stood at the dining room window of her father's house on the Battery. She was watching a great sailing vessel being guided into New York Harbor. It was nothing new; she had seen it being done many times before. But the sight of the small pilot boats tugging the mighty schooner into position never failed to fascinate her. Besides, she had a special interest in that ship.

On that late afternoon of August 27, 1789, a gentle breeze was blowing. The ship seemed to sway a little and then straighten again. Something about the strength of the masts and the majesty of the sails reminded her of her father, Doctor Richard Bayley.

He, too, was fearless and strong. Yet he often told her that she could twist him around her finger, just as the pilot boat could turn a sailing vessel big enough to battle the Atlantic.

She loved her father more than anyone else in the world. How distinguished he looked with the powdered hair, the lace cravat at his throat, the dark cloak that fell almost to the ground. His ready smile endeared him to everyone.

But today he had disappointed her. She was hurt and angry. He had made a promise, and he hadn't kept it. In the Bayley family a promise was a serious matter—something not to be broken.

Her fifteenth birthday party was just over, the last of the guests gone. Agatha, the cook, had made a special cake for the center of the table. The young housemaid, Hannah, who came from the north of Ireland, had asked if she could bake some cookies from a secret recipe. Everyone had liked them.

Elizabeth went over to the sideboard and looked at the gifts she had just received. A silk needlecase . . . a pink feather fan . . . an ivory cameo . . . a pair of cobwebby mittens . . . a golden thimble nestled in a walnut shell; a green satin pincushion handpainted by her best friend, Julia.

They are lovely, she thought, admiring each one. But even the presents couldn't make up for her disappointment. Her father had said he would look in on the party, even if it were for only a few minutes, but he hadn't come.

She crossed back to the window and looked out again. As she did so, she fingered the edge of the white fichu which draped the shoulders of her new silk gown. Her stepmother, Charlotte, had chosen the fabric for her.

Until today the only material she had worn had been woven by the spinning girls who came to the house two days a week and sang hymns while they worked.

In the late afternoon sunshine the schooner made a lovely picture. But Elizabeth was wondering about those aboard. Hannah had gone down hours ago to the wharf to meet her younger sister who had braved the long, tedious journey across the Atlantic by herself.

Everyone in the Bayley household liked the seventeen-year-old housemaid. When she had mentioned a younger sister who wanted to come to America, Mrs. Bayley had agreed to take her, also. There had been months of waiting for a passage, but at last the ship had arrived.

"I didn't close an eye all night, Miss Betty!"

Hannah had said in the morning. "I'm that excited about seeing my sister, I don't rightly know what I'm doing."

The pilot boats were leaving and a barge was coming alongside. Merchants and their wives and other important people would soon be coming down the gangway.

Later would come the immigrants who had been pronounced in good health and well enough to land. Elizabeth had seen such a group of immigrants only a short time before.

How tragic they had looked being herded ashore, some so weak that they had to be carried. Yet that day she had seen women fall on their knees in thankfulness that the long voyage was over. Some looked up, steadfast in the knowledge that here they would soon be making a new start.

The sound of children's feet running around overhead brought Elizabeth's thoughts back to her surroundings. Her small half-brothers and sisters were being put to bed.

Judging by the giggles and shrieks, it was going to be a long time before all seven of them would settle for the night.

For one reason Elizabeth was glad of this. It meant that by the time Hannah's sister reached the house the children would be asleep. That would leave her free to be the first to welcome her as soon as she arrived at the house.

Suddenly she remembered she hadn't told Agatha how delicious the birthday cake was! Running downstairs to the kitchen, she found the cook sitting in a rocking chair, snatching a few minutes' peace.

"Oh, Agatha," she said, "the cake was wonderful. Everyone loved the things you made."

"I'm glad, Miss Betty. But it was too bad your father couldn't be here. I know how much you wanted him to be." She shook her head thoughtfully. "A doctor's life is never his own."

Elizabeth said quickly, "I can't wait to see what Hannah's sister is like, can you?" She didn't want to discuss her disappointment over her father's broken promise.

"Well, it's to be hoped Hannah will settle down now," Agatha said, folding her arms across her ample chest. "This last week I couldn't get no good out of her."

Elizabeth walked away and went on upstairs. People were still coming ashore. Groups of men stood talking together and women carried babies, patting them to sleep. Bundles and boxes stood on the wharf, but there was no sign of Hannah.

"Betty!" came a sharp voice from over the bannister. "Why don't you come up? The children won't get into bed until you sing them to sleep. I want you up here immediately!" It was her stepmother calling.

"Yes, Mama, I'll come."

Elizabeth's temper was as quick as her mind. Once she would have answered sharply, but gradually she had overcome that fault.

She didn't obey immediately. She was thinking of her own mother and wishing the voice were hers.

She had died when Betty was not quite four years old. Elizabeth remembered the lonely feeling that seemed to follow her all over the house after her mother had gone. Now, almost twelve years later, she still missed her.

Elizabeth often lived over again in her mind that afternoon two years after her mother's death when her father had brought Charlotte Barclay to the house for the first time.

"This is your new mother," he had said, looking proudly at the beautiful girl he had married, and then at his daughter. "She is going to love you just like your own dear Mama did."

Charlotte had been kind to her. But as soon as her new halfbrothers and sisters began to arrive, Elizabeth felt she was no longer of any importance. The sense of belonging disappeared. She became more and more like a stranger in the house.

Only one person didn't change—her father. When he was home everything was wonderful. As Elizabeth grew older, it used to be her duty to bring him his slippers when he came in for afternoon tea.

He would stroke her hair and fuss over her as she bent down to put them on. Then he would draw her to him and ask what she had been thinking of since he last saw her.

But after Charlotte came, that little duty had been taken from her. Although her stepmother tried hard to make friends with her, something inside Elizabeth rebelled. She could never really love Charlotte, try as she would.

Elizabeth continued to look toward the Battery. Although she was only fifteen, she had seen many changes there. She remembered being taken for walks on the green lawns when she was a child, and later sitting under shady trees.

But now the docks bustled with life. Colored longshoremen struggled under heavy boxes; bales of goods were piled high along the wharf. Sometimes, when the wind was blowing in that direction, the smell of tobacco wafted through the rooms of the fashionable house where the Bayleys lived.

Elizabeth could remember, very faintly, the wild excitement when the flag of liberty was first unfurled at the Battery. She was just old enough to know something of what was going on.

Doctor Bayley, descended from an English family, was a Tory at heart. But he had given of his time and skill to the wounded—both British and American—and, when the war was over, he had sworn allegiance to the republic.

The new nation was fulfilling its promise to keep inviolate the Constitution. Now it was opening its doors to other nations who needed help.

As she watched by the window, an overwhelming sense of shame filled her. Coming off the ship were men, women, and children possessing nothing but the clothes they wore and a bundle of belongings tied in a scarf. And she, who possessed everything, had been angry because her father hadn't come to the party.

Now she realized he must be attending to the poor and sick immigrants.

Each one had to be examined by a doctor before being allowed to land. Several cases of yellow fever had been brought into the country unobserved before the expert Dr. Bayley had become health officer, but now the dread disease was usually diagnosed immediately.

How utterly selfish she had been! Elizabeth looked around the great room with its oak paneling, its Chippendale furniture, its family silver that graced the sideboard. How fortunate she was to live in such a beautiful house while others went homeless! In shame she laid her forehead against the window and closed her eyes tight. But two great tears came bursting through.

Dusk sifted over the water, turning the gold reflections into gray. A wail came from upstairs, then children's excited voices. One of them must have fallen out of bed.

Running toward the staircase Elizabeth called out, "I'm coming, Mama. I'm coming!" Half an hour later the whole brood of Bayleys was asleep.

The Bayleys usually dined at the fashionable hour of three o'clock in the afternoon, but, on account of the party, the order of things was changed.

They were awaiting Dr. Bayley's return. He was a busy man, so no one knew exactly when he would come home. They always waited until the last moment before sitting at the table.

"Another ten minutes," Mrs. Bayley said to Agatha, who always got into a "state" if food had to be kept hot.

Elizabeth admired her stepmother. She was just as beautiful now as the day when she first came to the house. She wore her clothes with charm and seemed to float when she walked. How pretty she looked in her gray gown, hooped at the sides, her white gauze cap and fichu.

Charlotte was sewing. There was always so much mending with seven children. "Betty," she said, without looking up, "you sew very nicely, but you'll never be accomplished if you don't work at your music. Then there's your French, to say nothing of your dancing."

"I should work harder at my lessons," Elizabeth agreed. "But I'd so much rather read than dance or speak French."

Charlotte Bayley disapproved. "You do altogether too much reading. You're always in your father's library with a book on your lap. I wouldn't object if you were studying your Bible. That . . ."

"Oh, but Mama, I do!" Elizabeth broke in. "I read it a great deal. I've learned many of the psalms by heart. They're so beautiful."

A smile crossed Charlotte's face. "I'm glad, dear. So glad. I love them, too. Perhaps we could read them together sometimes." Elizabeth knew her stepmother was a deeply religious woman.

Going to the window again and looking out, Elizabeth saw that by now a pale half-moon sailed through the sky. Lights from the schooner showed she was still swaying in the breeze.

"Surely Hannah can't be much longer. It seems hours and hours since the ship came in. I wonder if her sister will look like her."

"We've heard enough about the child. For months Hannah has talked of nothing else." Charlotte glanced up. "It will be wonderful to have another pair of hands to help with the washing and the mending."

The sound of horse's hoofs outside the house broke into their conversation.

"He's here at last. Your father's home." Charlotte put away her sewing basket. She stood up to smooth her gown.

Elizabeth ran down the hall to greet him.

"You look like a little queen," he said, taking off his cape. "Sorry I couldn't be at the party." He shook his head sadly. "So much sickness down at the wharf. I'm lucky to be home even now."

"Sorry to hear that, Father." The sadness in his eyes made her feel guiltier than before. She looked away from him toward the window in silence.

"It's too tragic for words," he said, kissing his wife, "to see those poor souls herded together on the boat like cattle."

"No yellow fever, I hope," Charlotte said.

Dr. Bayley stood still for a moment. When he spoke again his voice was grave. "One case. But . . . it was too late." He paused and sighed. "There was nothing I could do. The disease had gone too far. No one on board that ship would go near the poor girl. She's dead."

Elizabeth's heart seemed to stop for a minute. She watched her father's face. "It wasn't . . . it wasn't . . . ?" she gasped, afraid to finish the sentence.

Her father nodded. "Yes. It was Hannah's sister."

Chapter Two

INVITATION TO A BALL

On a warm September morning two years later, Elizabeth was sitting under a plum tree in her Uncle William's garden.

The sun through the leaves made quivering patterns on her riding habit and on the old stone seat as she leaned against the bark of the tree.

The tight-fitting jacket and the long skirt that young ladies wore in 1791 when they rode horseback looked very becoming. Her curls were tied back under a three-cornered hat. A fragrant odor of ripe plums filled the air.

Waiting for her friend Julia to come, she had been reading her leather-bound *Imitation of Christ* which her father had given her for her recent seventeenth birthday.

Julia and she had planned to go riding together. But Julia hadn't turned up. If she did come, Elizabeth was ready. But if she didn't, there was embroidery to do. She had brought it with her, just in case.

For nearly a month she had been staying with her aunt and uncle. Uncle William ran a school in the French town of New Rochelle. Every year since she could remember she had spent part of her holidays with them.

Julia, too, had a cousin who lived not far from Uncle William's house. The two seventeen-year-olds arranged their visits so that they could have fun together.

There were quite a number of boys and girls their own age who lived around New Rochelle. Often they went on picnics with someone's mother as chaperon. The boys fished while the girls chattered about gowns and beaux as they sat on the green lawns that sloped down to the water.

Looking straight ahead of her, Elizabeth could see the waters of Long Island Sound. What a lovely place this is, she thought. How fortunate I am to be able to come here every year.

The two girls were supposed to have started at

eight o'clock. But Elizabeth, knowing that her friend was seldom late, decided she must not be coming.

It was shadowed and cool under the plum tree in the wild part of her uncle's garden. She would sew and think.

"So, this is where you are!"

Surprised, Elizabeth dropped her spool of blue thread.

"Julia! Why, I'd given you up. I was sure you weren't coming." She thrust her book into the pocket of her riding habit and put her embroidery down on the seat.

"Sorry I'm late," Julia said. "Your aunt said I'd find you here. Do you still want to ride? Or do you feel like taking a stroll?"

A walk was something Elizabeth couldn't take in New York. There it wasn't safe or proper for young ladies to go out alone. Few of the streets were paved. When it rained, there were mudholes several inches deep. "Suppose we take the lane that leads to the hill. It's not very far."

The girls strolled along, clutching their skirts and lifting them slightly.

"I'm dying to hear all about your new ball-gown," Elizabeth said gaily.

"Oh," exclaimed Julia, "you should see the exquisite work the seamstress has put into it. You ought to ask your Mama if you can't have something like it. Tiny rosebuds embroidered in pink. Lovely!" Her eyes danced with happiness.

They discussed gowns and fans and slippers, although Julia did most of the talking. "Have you received your invitation to the Setons' ball yet?" she inquired.

"No, I haven't. Have you?"

"Not yet. But it's usually in November. There's lots of time, really. I just like to think about it." With a sigh and a half-smile Julia went on. "I can't help envying you a bit, Elizabeth."

"Why?"

"I'll tell you why. William Seton is in love with you."

Elizabeth laughed. "What an imagination you have!"

They reached the top of the hill. They sat down on a bench and rested. As Elizabeth put her head back against a branch, her long dark curls fell further over her shoulders.

"Your hair's prettier than any other girl's in our circle. Why don't you do more with it?" Julia was genuine in her admiration.

But Elizabeth was thinking of more important things. She bent forward and clasped her hands in her lap.

"You're so quiet and dreamy all the time," Julia said. "Are you in love?"

Elizabeth blushed. "Yes, I am. But I'm keeping

it a secret in my heart. I don't know if he loves me." She drew in her breath. "Love gives me such a warm, happy feeling. I want to share it. There are so many people who aren't loved. And when I hear my father talk about some old person who's friendless, well, I can't help getting upset because I'm not doing anything about it."

"But Betty, you are!" Julia said solemnly. "You seem to be always taking baskets of food to the poor. And the time you spend in those awful slums!" She shook her head. "I don't think you should. There's a hospital for sick people."

"But Julia, it was used as a barracks during the war. It's a terrible place. People would rather die than go there."

Julia was getting restless. "Oh, Betty, do cheer up. Life is so wonderful. Full of fun. I'm interested only in being in love and getting married. And it's no use pretending that all you want to do is fuss over lonely people—and nurse the sick!"

Elizabeth knew Julia wouldn't understand. "But I'm not pretending. I can't help being terribly sorry for them. It must be awful to have no one who cares."

Desperately Julia gave up. "You are a bit odd, you know. One minute gay. Next minute sad. I'd like to help, too. But it's so depressing . . . those dirty places they live in . . . ugh!"

"I guess we'd better be getting back," Elizabeth

suggested. "They'll be wondering where we are." She stood up and saw the choppy waters of the sound sparkling through the trees. "Do look at that pretty sailboat down there." She took Julia's hand. "Wouldn't you love to cross the great Atlantic one day and go to Europe?"

Julia laughed. "I'm quite sure there isn't a chance of that happening to me."

"I wonder if I ever shall," Elizabeth said dreamily.

They were nearing the house again. She could see her Aunt Anne gathering flowers in the garden. The stable boy sat on the whitewashed fence and whistled a merry tune.

When he saw the two girls approaching, he fetched Julia's chestnut saddle horse and helped her to mount. A moment later she was off at a gentle trot. "See you tomorrow," she called out. "Good-by."

As Elizabeth waved to her, she was unaware that her father was on his way by stagecoach to fetch her. There were two important reasons for this journey.

Having received an urgent message from an old wealthy patient who lived in New Rochelle, Dr. Bayley decided to visit him. He had once cured this man when everyone else had given him up. When a man gave so much of his time to the poor without fee, as Dr. Bayley did, a wealthy patient must be considered. With a large growing family, and servants to keep, expenses were great.

There was a second reason for his coming—something that would make Elizabeth proud of him.

After visiting his patient, he walked to his brother's home and pulled the bell. It was a small brown house, charming and unpretentious.

But inside was a welcome that might not be found in a larger mansion. Elizabeth was upstairs. She had changed from her riding habit into a blue calico gown. She was writing in her book which she called *Dear Remembrances*. Into this went all her inmost thoughts and prayers. Quill pen in hand, she listened, but she couldn't believe her ears. The voice sounded like her father's. It could not be. What reason would he have for coming?

"Bless the man," she heard Aunt Anne saying below in the hall. "If it isn't dear Richard. William! William! See who's here."

Elizabeth came running down the stairs and bumped into her uncle who came hurrying out of the library. "Father, how wonderful!"

A visitor from New York made a stir in such a small town, and, besides, the two brothers had not met in over a year. There were so many questions to be asked and answered.

After a hearty meal and a glass of Madeira wine, the doctor told his reasons for the surprise visit.

First, the rich patient. Then—and his smile was wide as he spoke—"Look upon not just Doctor Bayley, but Professor Bayley!"

Three pairs of eyes stared at him in amazement.

Laying his hand on Elizabeth's sleeve, he said, "I've accepted the post of first Professor of Anatomy at Columbia College in New York."

While her aunt and uncle were rejoicing, Elizabeth was afraid to speak lest she should dissolve in tears of happiness.

"I'm so proud," she said at last, getting up and kissing him. "How delighted Mama and the children must be." She drew in her breath. "I hope it doesn't mean you have to live at the college, does it?" She saw little enough of him as it was.

"Oh, no," he answered with a solemn face. "I'll be home to see that you practice your music and your French."

She knew he was teasing and smiled ruefully. "I confess I don't play the harpsichord any better today than I did when I was fifteen. But they do say," and she grinned impishly, "that I'm pretty good at dancing the minuet."

Her aunt leaned across the table and looked into Dr. Bayley's face. "Are you going to take our favorite niece back with you?" she asked. "If you do, there are going to be a few broken hearts in New Rochelle."

"We're all fond of her," Dr. Bayley said. "Not

because of her accomplishments, but because in her I see wisdom of soul!"

Elizabeth looked from one to the other, overcome with shyness. She wished her father would stop saying things like that. Making an excuse that she'd left her embroidery in the garden, she ran out of the room.

Wandering about among the flowers and trees, her thoughts were troubled. Her father was expecting great things of her. But what? Her mind seemed all mixed up. She couldn't be completely happy because she wasn't turning her spiritual desires into action. But where could she begin? She was standing so deep in thought that, when someone spoke to her, she jumped.

"I came to find you. I've something here that will please you."

Her father pulled a letter from his inside pocket and handed it to her. She opened it. It was a formal invitation, bidding Doctor and Mrs. Richard Bayley, and their daughter, Elizabeth Ann, to a ball at 65 Stone Street in November, to be given by Mr. and Mrs. William Seton.

She opened her eyes wide. "Are we going?"

"We've already accepted. We always enjoy ourselves at the Setons'. We've been friends for so many years. Besides, I wouldn't want you to miss the big event of the social season."

"Oh, no," cried Elizabeth, "it will be wonderful. And all the Seton boys are so nice." She would have liked to add . . . especially William, but that would be giving her secret away.

She noticed a faint smile on her father's face. "What makes you look so pleased?" she asked.

The doctor's smile grew broader. "Well, my dear, I met young William at the Merchant's Coffee House yesterday afternoon, and he made a point of coming over to my table for a chat. I'm inclined to think that he's in love with my little girl."

Elizabeth felt that skip of the heart that sent the blood to her cheeks. "Oh, what a tease you are, Father! Why should he be?"

"He's handsome and good. His father and I are old friends. He's well off; and why shouldn't he be in love with you?" Doctor Bayley took her arm, giving it a little pressure. "Isn't my Elizabeth like a tender bud, opening into flower?"

Slowly they walked back to the house.

Chapter Three

LOVE COMES GENTLY

AT the Seton ball Elizabeth wore a gown of yellow silk, with roses of the same color in her hair. Her father and Charlotte were particularly gay and happy. It was not often that all three of them could attend a social function together.

The wide staircase was flooded with light from crystal candelabra, and banks of flowers filled the air with faint perfume.

Their host and hostess greeted them graciously. Then Elizabeth went on with her father and mother into the ballroom.

The festivities were just beginning. From every corner of the great room came a rustle of movement and the hum of gay conversation.

Ladies danced to the music in green silk and in black velvet. Some wore diamonds in their hair. Others had long trains which fell gracefully behind them as they walked across the polished floor with their partners.

Mr. and Mrs. William Seton remained, smiling and greeting everyone, until the last guests had arrived. Then they mingled with the dancers. Amongst such elegant company it was hard to pick out Mr. Seton's white peruke or to distinguish his wife's cherry-colored gown, the silk for which had been brought over on one of his ships from France.

By eleven o'clock many of the refreshment tables were occupied. Elizabeth, on the arm of the oldest Seton boy, came into one of the small rooms seeking Julia. In her hand was a small bouquet of brown pansies and lilies-of-the-valley. They were charmingly arranged in a delicate lace holder. It was a token from William.

"If Julia's not here," he said, "I'll ask Mother if she was expected tonight, although it's quite possible we've just missed seeing her."

"How kind you are!" Elizabeth said. Then she remembered that William was never anything else but thoughtful.

Elizabeth couldn't help wondering. If Julia

were not at the ball, what could have prevented her from coming? For weeks and weeks they had been discussing it.

A long table placed near the wall in the refreshment room was filled with cakes, fruit, ices, and all kinds of wine. Servants stood behind it and waited upon the guests.

"William," Elizabeth said, "I'd love one of those delicious-looking ices . . . lemon, please."

They went to the table and took the ices that a white-haired manservant offered. Elizabeth noticed that he looked especially hard at her.

"Haven't I seen you before somewhere?" she asked him.

With a respectful bow of the head he answered, "Yes, Miss Elizabeth, you came and visited my poor sister when she had fever bad. I'll never forget your kindness. Never."

"And how is she now?"

"Fine. Fine—thanks to good Doctor Bayley and you."

William smiled at Elizabeth, but it was more than a smile. It was a look of deep admiration.

"Betty," he said, "you've made old Henry very happy tonight, remembering him. But then it seems you have a wonderful way of making everyone happy—especially me."

Her eyes met William's gaze as he escorted her

to a little gilt table. In each hand he was carrying an ice on a crystal plate.

"Shall we sit here and enjoy these?"

Young William Seton, the oldest of thirteen children, was six years older than Elizabeth. He was a much-traveled young man. Educated in England, he spoke French, Spanish, and Italian, and had visited most of the important cities of Europe. Besides, there was no town in America that he hadn't seen.

Originally the Setons came from a proud Scottish family who owned vast stretches of land, wooded glens and heather-covered hills. They lived in a manor house almost as big as a castle.

William's father was owner of a large shipping firm known as Seton, Maitland and Company. Young William was in partnership with him.

It was a simple matter for them to obtain objects of art for their beautiful house. The tapestries were from Florence, the chandeliers from Rome. Spanish carpets covered the floors.

Elizabeth was looking at William seated opposite her. How handsome he looks, she thought, in his high-backed coat of French cut, his powdered hair, and the Michelin lace at his throat. On his face was an expression she had never seen before. His eyes were full of love.

A lady in a cherry-colored gown came rustling

in from the ballroom to speak to them. It was Mrs. Seton.

"Betty, dear," she said, "I came to tell you that your father has been called away. A sick patient . . . quite seriously ill, I understand. Insists upon seeing him. Too bad . . . too bad."

"Oh, what a shame!" Elizabeth cried in genuine distress. "He so seldom has any fun."

Mrs. Seton smiled at her favorite son. "You'll be glad to escort Mrs. Bayley and Elizabeth home after the ball, won't you?"

"I am always at the command of the ladies," William replied. Then he added, "Mother, was Julia expected tonight? Elizabeth was asking for her."

"No, my dear. Julia went to visit friends in Philadelphia almost a week ago. The snow has been so heavy there that I understand no coach has been able to leave."

"She'll be so disappointed," Elizabeth said with a sigh.

When his mother returned to the ballroom, William looked across the little table straight into Elizabeth's eyes.

"Betty," he said, "I love you. I love you with all my heart."

For a long moment their eyes held. The words came as a surprise in spite of what her father had said. She had hoped that perhaps one day. . .

She felt her cheeks redden. "I love you, too," she said simply.

William took her hand across the table and kissed it. "I've been wanting to tell you since our first dance tonight. But I was afraid. I know I'm only one of the young men in this room who have lost their hearts to you."

"Well, if there are . . . which I doubt . . . I'm completely unaware of them."

His eyes were grave. "If you'll only give me hope, I shall be the happiest man in the world."

What will his mother say? she was thinking. Elizabeth knew that William was not so robust as the other Seton boys and girls, and that, perhaps because of this, he was her favorite.

She whispered to him, "I do love you, William, but you must think about your mother. What will she say?"

"She knows how I feel about you. She couldn't help but know! Elizabeth, will you be mine?" Elizabeth gave him a little nod of acceptance. "I am yours, William."

Those words were determining their whole future. How lucky I am, she thought. How fortunate . . . how blessed.

The music was beginning again. They went back into the ballroom. As they danced, they seemed lost in each other. "When is the best time to speak to your father?" he asked. "You see, like every other man in love, I'm impatient. I want his formal permission to call on you."

"If he can spare the time, he usually comes home in the afternoon for tea."

"Then that's when I shall call."

Elizabeth didn't want to dance any more. "Couldn't we sit here for a while?" she suggested, finding a quiet place in the far corner of the room. "We have so many things to talk about."

It was strange. She had known William for a long time, but this was the first serious talk she'd had with him. She could hardly believe she would be his wife. But he had said so. And now she felt she could listen to him forever.

"Dearest, have you ever wished you could go to England or to France? Or, maybe, to Italy?" William asked.

"Oh, yes! Many times. I'd love to see where my father's family lives. About Paris, I'm not so sure. It sounds so terribly frivolous. But Italy . . . I think that must be beautiful."

"I hoped you'd say that about Italy." He looked down at her beside him. With a rush of tenderness he added, "I want to be the one to take you. I want to show you off to my dearest friends."

"And who are they?"

"The Filicchis of Leghorn. You see, our ships ply mostly between that port and New York. Our business associates are two brothers, Antonio and

Filipo Filicchi. But really we are friends first and partners afterwards."

So now she knew who they were. Their names had been mentioned so many times at 65 Stone Street. It was unbecoming for a girl to question about business, so she had never asked.

Charlotte Bayley was coming towards them. A faint frown between her eyebrows meant she was in a mood. "It's getting late," she said, looking at Elizabeth.

William rose to his feet, smiling graciously at the woman he hoped would be his mother-in-law one day.

"Your mother said you would kindly escort us home since Dr. Bayley isn't here," Charlotte told him.

"I'm always at your service," he replied courteously. Soon he was taking them to his waiting carriage.

Mr. and Mrs. William Seton kissed Elizabeth good night on both cheeks, something they had never done before. Her heart warmed to them.

As the carriage door was opened, William whispered, "How can I wait until tomorrow, darling?"

The distance was all too short. Only a few streets separated the two homes, but, happily, the snow and the narrow cobblestone roads made progress slow.

When they reached home and the front door

was closed behind them, Elizabeth went quickly to her bedroom. She listened until the sound of wheels on the snow died away. Hannah had put out her nightgown and robe for her. The fire had gone out, and the room was chilly. But her heart was warm, and the lighted candles gave a cosy glow.

She stepped to the window and looked out on the quadrangle in front of the house. A light snow was falling again.

"Fancy me, Elizabeth Ann Bayley, going to be married!" She pressed the velvet-soft pansies to her lips. This bouquet must be kept forever and ever. "I love you, William, I love you," she whispered half aloud.

Still wearing her warm hood and cape, she looked in the mirror. "One day I'm going to be Mrs. William Seton," she told her reflection. But tonight no one should share her secret.

Charlotte came into the room looking worried. "Your father's not home yet. Tired as I am, I cannot sleep until he comes in."

Elizabeth looked at the clock on the mantel. Almost three-thirty in the morning. "I'll wait up with you, Mama."

"No, thank you." She kissed her stepdaughter good night. "It's just that the streets are full of footpads and cutthroats. It's not safe to be out." As she reached the door she turned and said:

"Never marry a doctor. You're lucky if you ever know where he is, day or night!" She closed the door behind her.

Strange, Elizabeth thought. Charlotte has never mentioned marriage to me before. She longed to tell her stepmother. But that little invisible barrier that so often came between them prevented her from doing so.

She began to unhook her yellow gown. She had said yes to William, but she'd promised him to have her decision formally announced before he left for Italy.

If only he didn't have to cross the Atlantic, she thought. But Elizabeth knew how much his father depended upon him to run his affairs at Leghorn.

Slipping into her dimity nightgown, she knelt beside her bed.

"Dear God, thank you for William," she whispered.

The clock in the tower of the North Dutch Church chimed four before she fell asleep.

The poplar trees on the Battery put forth their leaves again. It was the spring of 1793.

A week before William was to sail for Italy, the Bayleys gave a supper party and announced the engagement of Elizabeth Ann to William Magee Seton.

New York society showered the happy couple

with glad messages. Only the thought of having to say good-by so soon overshadowed the happiness of the newly engaged pair.

The day came when they must take leave of one another. While William's parents chatted with the Bayleys at the wharf, and the sailors loaded cargo into the ship's hold, William gave his fiancée a parting gift.

Her heart pounded as Elizabeth opened the little package. There, in its velvet lining, winking in the sun, was a gold locket studded with diamonds. Inside the top of the box were the words *Labouchère, Paris*.

Elizabeth gasped. "Oh, William! Oh, how exquisite!" Never before had she owned anything half so beautiful. More words simply wouldn't come.

The sloop, flying the flag of Seton, Maitland and Company, soon set sail with William aboard. The two families remained on the wharf until the masts melted into the sky. Elizabeth felt as if the whole world had disappeared and had left her standing there.

"Dear Julia," Elizabeth wrote in December of that year, "William and I are going to be married on January 25, 1794. The Right Reverend Samuel Provoost, Protestant bishop of New York, will officiate at Trinity Church. We want you to be matron of honor. . . ."

Elizabeth was still not used to addressing her best friend as Mrs. Scott. But Julia was married now and lived in Philadelphia.

The usual flurry of presents, and people coming and going with bolts of delicate materials, turned the Bayley house into a frenzy of excitement. But through it all Elizabeth was aware that neither gifts nor gowns could fill her with complete happiness. Only spiritual joy could do that. In William's love for her they had found it together.

The wedding day finally dawned. Trinity Church, newly rebuilt, was almost filled with smiling relatives. The small Seton children sat on one side and the small Bayleys on the other.

Now she was walking modestly up the aisle on the arm of her father. People nodded to her from both sides. Doctor Provoost, portly and dignified, was there to officiate.

Julia, and Elizabeth's young sister-in-law, Rebecca, were almost as excited as the bride.

When William placed the ring upon her finger, she knew that their lives were unalterably bound together, firm in each other's love.

Radiant, Elizabeth sent up prayers to heaven that she might be worthy of such happiness.

Chapter Four

STAY BESIDE ME, ALWAYS

THE next seven years were happy ones for Elizabeth and William. At first they lived with the Setons at 65 Stone Street, sharing the house with William's younger sisters and brothers.

Rebecca, Harriet, and Cecilia were devoted to Elizabeth. Seldom was a new sister-in-law welcomed so warmly into a family.

When their first child, Anna, was born, the young Setons were living in a house on Wall Street.

Three more children came to the happy household—William, Richard, and Catherine. The boys were always called by their full names, but Catherine became Kitty. Anna's name became longer. She was called Annina, which, in Italian, means Little Anna.

Dr. Bayley was a proud grandpa.

"This little darling," he once said, when Annina was old enough to sit on his knee," has more intelligence in her sweet face than any other in the world."

Elizabeth would scold. "You're spoiling her, Father. I can't get any good out of any of the children after you've been here."

But she was only teasing. Nothing pleased her more than to have her father visit them and play games in the nursery. When Dr. Bayley was there, the children would run around him shrieking and giggling until Grandpa was exhausted.

"The wildest colts make the best horses," he said when Elizabeth tried to quiet them.

Not only her own children romped through the house. William's young brothers and his sisters, Rebecca, Harriet, and Cecilia came, too. Six-year-old Annina called them "Aunt," but it was only a joke. Harriet and Cecilia were not so very much older than she.

Sometimes Elizabeth's stepmother brought some of her own brood over to visit. Guy Carlton Bayley was her oldest son and Elizabeth's favorite half brother.

Snap the Whip was a favorite game. Sometimes the grownups joined in the fun and made more noise than the children.

Young William was getting old enough to be interested in watching the workmen on the Battery strengthening the flagstaff with planks and masonry. Anything to do with the sea he loved; he never missed the comings or goings of ships.

Dressed in their nankeen suits, their trousers gathered at the ankles, William pretended to be a sailor while Richard imitated Grandpa Seton, making believe he was an important business man.

Sometimes they would be lamplighters with imaginary tinderboxes, or watchmen with shiny hats, calling out the hours and the weather.

At bedtime, after Elizabeth had heard their prayers, the children waited for their father to tell them stories. They loved to hear about the wonderful places he had visited.

Annina, being the oldest, came and sat on one of the four-poster beds in the younger children's room and listened. She loved to dream of faraway places, wondering if she would ever see them.

When the story was over, William would carry Annina to her own room and plant a kiss on top of her dark curls. Once he told her that she was as beautiful as her mother.

One night when William came home and Elizabeth ran to meet him as usual, she noticed how pale he looked. There were two unnaturally rosy patches around his cheek bones. When she took his hands, they were burning. She was frightened. It was the beginning of an illness which was to recur many times during the next year.

It was only when William was well again and able to return to his office that she went back to her work in the slums. Hannah had begged Mrs. Bayley, when Elizabeth was married, to allow her to be housemaid to the young Setons. She often accompanied Elizabeth when she walked through the unpaved swamps to the shacks that housed the poor.

The rickety dwellings were surprisingly near the elegant houses along the Battery. Sometimes William's sister, Rebecca, went along with her, too. They braved the scorn that some of their friends made no attempt to hide.

Some of the shacks had no windows, and the odor of the places was sickening, but Elizabeth never spared herself. She conquered her reluctance to go in, remembering there were helpless people awaiting the sound of her footsteps.

Once she sat at the bedside of an old Frenchwoman. The room was lighted by a candle. The patient's breathing was short and irregular, and her eyes burned with a kind of excitement.

The sick woman repeated the same words incessantly, looking imploringly into Elizabeth's face. It was impossible to understand what she mumbled.

Perhaps if I bent closer to her, Elizabeth thought, I could make out what she wants. She leaned farther over the bed, and, as she did so, the old woman's wrinkled hand came up and took hold of something. It was the small gold crucifix Elizabeth always wore on a chain around her neck.

"Ah, *merci . . . merci!*" Just to hold the cross had soothed her. She smiled faintly and seemed content. Her breathing became less rapid. Before Elizabeth left, she said to the old woman, "I shall come tomorrow and see you again."

The peace that the sight of the little crucifix had brought made a great impression upon her. She would always remember the look of faith in the Frenchwoman's eyes.

When Elizabeth returned to her comfortable home, she thanked God that she was strong enough to do the work for the poor that she loved and to run her household smoothly at the same time.

She always managed to look fresh and sweet presiding over the table when William invited important guests to dine. The fact that she had often spent hours at a meeting to discuss a charitable project was never mentioned.

"Now, dear," Dr. Bayley said to her one day, "admit that you're doing too much. This organization you're so interested in . . . this . . . what's the name of it . . . ?"

"The Society for the Relief of Poor Widows and Small Children."

"Well, whatever it's called . . . you're not over-strong yourself, and you're such a little thing. Well, I'm going to speak to William about it. It's too much. . ."

"No . . . no, Father." Elizabeth interrupted. "As it is now . . ." She smiled. "He has a special name for you. He calls you Mr. Monitor!"

Dr. Bayley laughed. "Oh, very well! I won't say anything."

One morning he rode over to tell his daughter the latest news in the Bayley family. "We're going to move to Staten Island. The new quarantine station has been completed, and I've been appointed Inspector General of the Health Department. I can't help being immensely pleased."

Elizabeth greeted this news with mixed feelings. She was proud and happy that her father's brilliance had been recognized. But oh, how she was going to miss him.

"It's wonderful," she said, giving him a big kiss.

Through the window came the sound of child-ish voices. Dr. Bayley looked out. Annina and roly-poly Kitty were holding hands, advancing and retreating as they sang:

> "I came to see Miss Jenny O'Jones,
> Miss Jenny O'Jones, Miss Jenny O'Jones
> I came to see Miss Jenny O'Jones
> And how is she today?"

Dr. Bayley smiled and shook his head. "I'm going to miss those darling grandchildren, bless them," he said.

Soon a more serious matter was to fill Elizabeth's mind. William suddenly became dreadfully worried. His father's death three years ago had put great responsibility on his shoulders. Then he had taken it in his stride. But now it was as if some shadow were threatening their happiness. Elizabeth begged him to tell her what the trouble was, but he only shook his head and was silent. She was soon to learn.

England and France were at war. The French Revolution was coming to an end, although terrible massacres were still taking place. England had ordered the French minister to leave the country. This resulted in war.

All shipping was affected. News traveled slowly but surely. Pirates roamed the high seas. Suddenly, and without warning, the whole Seton family was faced with the possibility of ruin. William had seen it coming.

It was not long before word reached them that one of their ships had been seized. Within a month a second had been added to their list of disasters. The Seton fortune was shattered.

All William could do was to stare out of the window into the gathering darkness. He was unable to cope with his tremendous losses, and he barely turned when Elizabeth spoke to him.

Taking up the reins, Elizabeth worked far into the night planning economies. She couldn't let Hannah go, but she would have to dismiss two of the other servants. Entertaining, clothes, housekeeping bills all could be cut down.

Holding an oil lamp in her hand when she had finished, she crept upstairs and stood beside William's bed. He was not asleep. As soon as he saw her, he looked up, taking her hand convulsively.

"Elizabeth!" he said. "Elizabeth . . . without you I couldn't go on. I wouldn't want to live." He pressed her fingers to his lips, almost reverently.

"We must be thankful for our love, William. We'll battle this thing through together."

Their trials were only beginning.

In August, 1801, Charlotte sent a messenger with a note to Elizabeth. It read: "Come at once. Your father is ill and asking for you."

Her heart began to beat furiously. How could she leave William now? Tensely she regarded the messenger. "I'll come. I'll be there as soon as I can."

With all possible haste she took the ferry boat that plied between New York and Staten Island. When she reached her father's house in the rain, she was expecting to find him in bed. To her delight he was sitting in his armchair by the window, sipping wine. Charlotte and he were watching the sunset as a rainbow faded into it.

"Oh! you came . . . you came," he cried out joyfully when he saw her.

She threw her arms around his neck and kissed him. Charlotte gave her one of her rare caresses. "You're always so good," she said. "Always dependable."

Before her father went to sleep that night, he called Elizabeth to his bedside. "Now that we are alone a moment," he said in a slow, shaky voice, "there are the keys to my desk." He pointed to a table near by. It sounded so final, as if he knew it were the last time he would see her. "All my important papers are in there. I want you to take care of things. Charlotte has the children to look after . . . she hasn't much of a business head . . ."

The next night, after a long spell of delirium, Dr. Bayley died.

Later, when Charlotte was able to speak about it, Elizabeth asked her what had caused her father's illness.

"A surgeon came late at night, just as your father had settled into his slippers. It was a week ago. He hadn't been well for a long time. 'Your advice is wanted, Richard,' said the other doctor. 'We don't know what to do . . . it's a needy family.' "

Elizabeth nodded. "Knowing him, I can guess the rest."

"If only I had insisted that he should not go. He had complained of pains in his head and in his stomach. I had no idea. . ." She was too overcome to go on.

Her father's death was Elizabeth's first personal sorrow. It was so difficult to be courageous, but she must be, for Charlotte's sake. She had not told her stepmother of her own troubles. She would know soon enough about Seton, Maitland and Company.

It was the first time she'd been away from her children. When she returned it was evening. William had not yet come home from his office. All the children, except Annina, were in bed.

She had been away from home only a few days, and yet it seemed like weeks. "Have they been good?" she asked Hannah upstairs. She bent over them, feeling a rush of love for each sleepy head.

"Like little angels, ma'am," Hannah told her. "But the master hasn't been eating well. He's never the same if you're not at the table with him."

Elizabeth sat at the window waiting for William to come home. She loved the new house they had rented at 8 State Street, but worry about William's health gnawed at her contentment. It was two years since Dr. Bayley's death, and still William's health grew worse.

When he came in, Elizabeth was shocked at his appearance. He looked haggard and worn. Worry was quickly undermining his health.

She made a decision even before he spoke to her. She would call a physician that night. "Your news is bad . . . I can tell," she said. "Whatever it is, we must share it, William."

He sank onto the sofa in utter despair, his face between his hands. "Two more of our ships have been seized by pirates. We have only one left. There's no way of getting back our losses. Poverty stares us in the face."

"And the Filicchis . . . are they ruined, too?"

"No," William said. "They are wealthy bankers, as well. We had only ships."

Elizabeth's spirit never flagged. Putting aside her own grief, she knew she mustn't let William despair.

"Something will turn up," she said. "You're so wonderfully clever, so resourceful." She knelt beside him, lifting her face to his, trying to comfort him.

"Stay beside me always . . . always, my darling," William said.

Moments later Elizabeth was bending over her husband's prone figure. He had collapsed in a dead faint.

Hannah was dispatched in a carriage to fetch the family doctor.

"Stupid of me," William said when he recovered, lifting himself weakly on one elbow. "How did I get here?"

When the doctor came, Elizabeth stood back to allow him to make his examination. It seemed to go on for hours, eternities.

Elizabeth awaited the verdict. The doctor's fingers opened and closed, betraying his agitation.

"William must have a complete change of scenery. I would suggest . . . Italy, perhaps."

Elizabeth gasped. "Italy?"

"The Filicchis," William said. "They'd be glad to have us."

The doctor looked at Elizabeth. "You'll go with him, of course."

She thought for just a moment of her little ones —Annina and the boys, Kitty and little Rebecca, only a year old.

"Of course," she replied, as if crossing the Atlantic were nothing at all. "Long ago William promised to take me."

The doctor pursed his lips, nodding his head.

"Good. Better write to your friends in Italy tonight. It will take weeks to get an answer . . ."

"Wait a moment, doctor," Elizabeth said quickly. "My half brother, Guy Carlton, is leaving soon to join the Filicchi banking firm in Leghorn. It's like a miracle that he should be going just at this time. I'll send a message to him to give to the Filicchis."

"Then the problem is solved." The doctor spoke in a matter-of-fact voice. But Elizabeth knew he was far from calm.

She went with him to the front door. "What do you think? You think maybe . . ." She faltered, frightened by the shadow of something in the doctor's eyes.

"William is a very sick man, my dear. Keep him from worrying. No physical exertion. I know I can rely on you. I'll call again in a day or two."

The front door closed and she leaned against it, her head thrown back, trying valiantly to be calm.

"Elizabeth!"

"Yes, darling. I'm coming."

William smiled and held out his hand for her to take. "I just wanted to tell you . . . how much I love you."

Chapter Five

THE SAILING OF THE SHEPHERDESS

On a blustery October afternoon, the Setons, standing on the wharf, exchanged last-minute messages with friends and relatives.

"Be sure Bec doesn't get into drafts. She takes cold easily," Elizabeth warned.

Harriet nodded. "I'll take care of her. Don't worry. And be sure to write. We'll hardly be able to wait until we hear from you."

"You've got those documents for the Filicchis, haven't you?" asked a clerk from the Seton office who had come to see William off.

"Don't stay away too long," cried Rebecca.

A small commercial brig called the *Shepherdess* was going to take Elizabeth and William from New York Harbor to Leghorn. Usually every ship carried a few passengers as well as freight. But now nobody traveled for pleasure. Too many pirates from the Barbary States prowled the high seas.

The Setons couldn't afford to take more than one child, so Annina, being the oldest, went with them. She was nearly nine, blithe and gay, with charming manners. Today she felt she was quite a young lady. It was on account of a lovely gift— two new dresses which her doting aunts, Harriet and Rebecca, had given her. They were short frocks that reached halfway between her knees and her ankles. From under them white pantalets peeped out.

Grandma Bayley had made a special trip from Staten Island the day before to bring a large yellow straw hat for Annina. It tied under the chin with a wide satin ribbon. No wonder she was happy.

Elizabeth had warned Annina. "These things must be kept for good. Now we must go back to the simplicity of the Revolution. New clothes were scarce then. But now it is just that we cannot afford them."

As the time drew near for departure, there was much embracing and many tears. Everyone loved the young pair who were forced to leave behind their four young children.

The winds blew sharply as a small, leaky boat put out from the Battery towards the ship. "Goodby and God bless you!" The words came back, carried over the water.

Soon the Setons were boarding the *Shepherdess*. Those lingering on the wharf appeared now to be no more than black specks. Elizabeth's heart sank when she thought of little William's yellow curls and of Richard's saucy smile. The children would be going to bed now—Kitty and Bec, too.

Various members of the family had promised to look after the children in the absence of their parents. Elizabeth had been forced to bite her lips to keep the tears back as they were fetched and taken away.

Once the *Shepherdess* was afloat, Annina's eyes sparkled. A moment later she asked, "What's that smoke against the sky?"

William answered. "That's fog. Looks like we'll have rough going."

For several days the ship battled against head winds. Great splashes of spray swept the decks, covering the hatches and pouring into the hold.

The captain of the ship, Mr. O'Brien, and his wife made the voyage as pleasant as possible. Annina adored their eighteen-month-old baby. She sang her to sleep or played with her every day.

The Setons' cabin was small and gloomy. Two whale-oil lamps and a single porthole high above the built-in bunks were all they had for light.

One night a clashing squall roared outside. Lightning cracked open the skies. The ship shuddered and reeled. It was the first time Elizabeth had ever faced the terrors of a storm at sea.

In her bunk, with Annina half-asleep in her arms, Elizabeth pressed her face close to the frightened child and closed her arms tightly around her.

"Hush, darling," she whispered, "remember God is watching over us. The worst that can happen will not harm us."

Morning came. The sky never seemed so blue. The storm was forgotten. William, an experienced sailor, was already looking better. The tossing of the ship didn't bother him. But Elizabeth and Annina were thankful to have a kind stewardess to attend them.

While William slept on deck, Elizabeth, sitting beside him, wrote letters. Sometimes the pitching of the decks made this almost impossible. Then she would read her *Imitation of Christ* and learn passages of it by heart.

Once when William awoke from a doze he looked up at her and asked, "How's my little manager?"

Elizabeth smiled. She knew what he was referring to. When William's father had died, she had gone over to Mrs. Seton's house and had run it for her, as well as managing her own.

"Oh, I'm not such a good manager as you think," she said. "It's just that my father taught me self-reliance when I was a child."

"We'll soon be at the Western Isles, Mrs. Seton." Elizabeth was startled. She hadn't seen anyone approaching. The voice belonged to Captain O'Brien. "We're halfway over now. Hasn't been a bad trip at all."

Elizabeth wondered what a bad trip must be like. For days she had found it hard enough to fight her way up and down the reeling decks.

"I'll be glad when we reach Leghorn, just the same!" she said firmly.

"Feeling better, Mr. Seton? You've got to get a little more sun," said the captain, and his hand closed hard on William's shoulder. He looked at Elizabeth. "Better hurry with your letters, ma'am. We expect to meet some vessel hourly. She will take your letters home."

This was wonderful news. As Elizabeth had said to Rebecca, Harriet, and Cecilia in her letter, "a quire of paper couldn't tell you all I want to say."

She hoped she hadn't forgotten anyone, knowing how much a letter from abroad meant. There was a long one going to the Reverend Dr. Henry Hobart, Anglican rector of St. Paul's Church in New York City. He was a very dear friend and the spiritual director of the Bayley and Seton families.

The friendly stewardess was coming towards them, a worried expression replacing her usual smile. "I think you should come, Mrs. Seton," she said. "Annina's not feeling too well."

The child had been suffering from a cold and cough, but suddenly she began to whoop. "I'm afraid she's taken the whooping cough from Captain O'Brien's baby."

Days and restless nights passed. The childhood ailment was making Annina thin and listless. William, who had been enjoying much better health, suddenly took a turn for the worse.

"What a wonderful nurse you are, Mrs. Seton," said the stewardess, bringing into the cabin some soup for the invalids.

Elizabeth's mouth quivered as she looked at William. The hollows under his cheekbones were growing deeper every day. A cough racked his chest as he lay propped up in his bunk. Annina was unable to keep any food down. Between the two, Elizabeth was almost at her wit's end.

That night, as she was preparing for bed, she heard stifled sobs coming from under the blanket where Annina lay. "What's the matter, darling?"

The child rolled herself into a ball and sobbed harder. "I miss Kitty . . . and Richard . . . and Father's so sick. Is he . . . going to die?"

Poor little thing, thought Elizabeth. It hadn't been any fun for her. "Soon you'll have the Filicchi children to play with. Perhaps they'll meet the boat. They'll be excited to have a little American girl for a friend."

Annina stopped crying and soon fell asleep.

The long voyage was nearing its end. The *Shepherdess* had passed Gibraltar. With all the sea air and the sunshine, William was no better. Each morning Elizabeth awoke hopefully. Each night her heart sank.

"Help us, dear Lord," she prayed, "for Thou art our Father."

The ship was now in the bay, and the blue waters of the Mediterranean sparkled. A lone bird in the sky was flying across the sun.

That night Elizabeth went to sleep with a prayer in her heart. As if in answer, she had a strange dream. She seemed to be climbing a great mountain in utter darkness and alone.

When she was near the top, a voice said, "Take courage! There is a beautiful green hill on the other side, and on it an angel waits for you."

It was so vivid that Elizabeth could never forget it. Could this mean that, having passed through a hazardous journey, she would find happiness in Italy? Would that be the other side of the hill?

The captain's wife was talking to Elizabeth. "It's really been a lovely voyage," she said. "Even with the storms and the dead calms, at least we were not sighted by pirates!"

Just at sundown, on November 18, the *Shepherdess* sailed past the lighthouse into the harbor of Leghorn. The long journey was over.

A great stone fortress protected the entrance to the port. From the courtyard below came familiar music. A brass band was playing American tunes. What a wonderful welcome!

Annina, in anticipation of all the fun that had been promised, skipped around excitedly. Dressed in one of her new gowns and pantalets, the straw hat tied under her chin like a large poke bonnet, she felt quite a lady of fashion.

"Hold still, sweetheart," Elizabeth said, "or you'll begin coughing again."

Over the sound of hawsers splashing into the water came the sound of church bells.

"They're ringing the Angelus," said William, who had been in Italy many times before.

The excitement of arrival had put color into his cheeks. His eyes were bright with the thought of meeting his best friends, the Filicchis. "Look, dearest, they're here. The Filicchis are here!"

Elizabeth, seeing her favorite half brother on the wharf, cried out, "Carlton!" Her heart was beating as if it would burst. "Carlton!"

A small boat came alongside. Out of it stepped

a man in uniform. He handed some papers to Captain O'Brien and engaged him in conversation.

They were so close to the wharf now that Elizabeth opened her arms wide and was about to reach out to Carlton when something happened. A fierce-looking guard had stepped forward and was thrusting a pole between them.

"No touch! No touch!" he shouted angrily.

Captain O'Brien explained. "I'm terribly sorry this should have happened, but there's nothing I can do. You cannot land. The *Shepherdess* sailed from New York without a health certificate. On account of Mr. Seton's illness, the authorities will not allow you to land. There is a scare of yellow fever!"

"Not the Lazaretto!" William's face was deathly pale. "Does this mean . . . the Lazaretto?" He put a protective arm around Elizabeth and grabbed hold of Annina's hand, pulling her close to him.

Captain O'Brien's expression was one of distress. "I'm afraid it does, Mr. Seton." He shook his head. "I'm entirely helpless. They won't listen to me!"

Without further questioning . . . without speaking to the Filicchis . . . without explanation to Carlton, the three Setons with their trunk found themselves being towed behind another boat out to sea again. They were being taken like prisoners to a pesthouse. People with infectious diseases were kept there in quarantine. It was called the Lazaretto and was built on an island out at sea.

William's tears rose up with such violence that his whole body shook. The shock had rendered him speechless.

Annina clung to her mother in absolute terror.

"We'll all be together, darling. Maybe this is a big mistake," said Elizabeth, trying to comfort the child while inside her own heart was breaking.

For a full hour they were towed through the water. They reached an ugly stone building. It looked like a prison. A bell clanged out from somewhere, and the chains across the channel were let down.

They were told to get out of the boat.

"Assist me. Let me lean on you, Elizabeth," William whispered. "I don't know if I can climb those steps."

He looked as if he were about to faint. A coughing spell left him panting and in great pain. Annina, hungry, tired, and disappointed, wept.

Even Elizabeth's strong spirit began to waver. What an end to the journey! But as she saw the fearful distress of those she loved, her father's words came to her. "Face life fearlessly, with eyes upward." Yes, she thought, William and Annina are looking to me for comfort. I mustn't let them down.

The room in which they were to spend possibly

a month was bare, cold, high-ceilinged. The floor, made of brick, had not so much as a piece of matting on it.

Elizabeth's thoughts flew back to the immigrants in New York. How little she had dreamed then that she would one day be imprisoned in such a place.

Three mattresses, those they had used on board ship, had been thrown into the boat with them. These were flung on top of boards by the Capitano, who was the officer in charge of the Lazaretto. By reason of his office, he had to stay in quarantine with the Setons until the health laws would permit their landing in Leghorn.

Outside the fortress-like building, a sentry in cocked hat and military uniform paced up and down carrying a long rifle.

The Capitano, obviously not enjoying his task, made himself known and, smiling, wished the Setons a good night's sleep. Then he disappeared. About an hour later he returned, bringing the trunk.

Annina began to cry again from hunger. "What do we do about food?" Elizabeth asked William.

The Capitano, coming in once again, answered the question. "Your friends, Signor Filicchi and his lady, sent you these," he said. He produced three warm eggs, a bottle of wine, and some sticks of bread. "I hope you won't be cold. Perhaps your friends will send some blankets tomorrow." Then he left them for the night. Elizabeth waited until William and Annina were asleep. Then wearily she flung herself down, beyond tears.

The crashing of the sea against the stone walls kept her from sleeping. The strange dream that came to her when the ship was in the Bay of Gibraltar . . . was this prison the dark mountain she was to climb? Would there be a green field somewhere on the other side?

After a while she rose. Kneeling in the moonlight that came through the high double-barred window, she prayed for spiritual strength.

"Dear God, give me the humility to understand the meaning of the suffering that has come upon us so unexpectedly."

Chapter Six

THE OTHER SIDE OF THE HILL

THE stone walls of the Lazaretto confined the
Setons for almost a month. They were never warm.
An odor of decay came up from the brick floor
splotched with green dampness. A small charcoal
fire was the only heat provided for them. The
fumes from it made both William and Annina
cough.

Sometimes the child jumped rope to keep warm,
using the cord that had been tied around the trunk.
Hoping to get William to laugh, Elizabeth joined
in with her.

If adversity is the test of friendship, the Filicchis proved it. They sent blankets, cough syrups, and all kinds of delicacies to coax the invalid's appetite.

One day a long narrow parcel arrived for Annina. She was wildly excited. A piece of green material poked through where the wrapping paper was torn.

"Mama! Oh, Mama, what can it be?"

She was putting off the happiness of opening it as long as possible. "Gracious, child," said Elizabeth, "I'm as anxious to know what it is as you are."

A big rag doll lay in the box. It had golden hair and a long green dress. She picked it up and hugged it to her. "Look Father! Isn't she lovely?"

Most of the days were spent in lessons for Annina and reading the Bible. Sometimes while William dozed Elizabeth wrote her *Dear Remembrances*. Expressing thoughts to her friends passed the long hours. To Julia she wrote, "Remember when you and I went on horseback as far as Pembroke? I said I would gladly live on earth forever. All that is changed. Not for all the joys together would I be tempted to live here, except as a pilgrim."

Once a great disturbance broke out in the Lazaretto. The room next to theirs sounded as if it were filled with madmen. All night fists were beating against the walls. Swearing, threatening, and murderous yells rose above the sound of the waves.

The Capitano told the Setons next morning that a group of Greek and Turkish sailors had been rescued from a shipwreck.

"How happy we are," Annina said, "in comparison to those men. We, at least, have mattresses and dry clothes. And we don't quarrel."

The Capitano said one day to Elizabeth, "I've seen strong men take their lives when they've been imprisoned here. And you . . . you're so grateful for the smallest comfort."

Once they were allowed to speak to Carlton through an iron grille.

"We'll have lots of fun soon," he called out to Annina, who was standing on a chair trying to see her uncle.

Worry kept Elizabeth from sleeping. If William were going to be an invalid, what about their future? What was to become of their five little ones?

As soon as she tried to close her eyes, the bells that announced the hours, night and day, would ring out like a knell for departing spirits. Often she wondered if their clanging noise and the pounding of the waves against the walls would haunt her forever.

She thought so often about little Bec . . . her baby. It was hard to miss all her pretty new ways. Her only consolation was to send prayers winging westward, like little white gulls.

When at last the time came for their release

from the Lazaretto, they stood with their trunk waiting for the rowboat. The Capitano, with his cocked hat under his arm, bowed respectfully and bade them Godspeed. The sentry smiled and said he was sorry, for his own sake, to see them leave.

"Thank you for all you've done for us." Elizabeth spoke from the bottom of her heart.

The Capitano handed her into the boat that was to take them back to Leghorn. The chains of the Lazaretto were finally let down, and the oarsman began to row.

A great crowd had gathered on the wharf to greet them. "Here they come!" shouted an English voice, and the people pressed forward eagerly.

It was like a dream to Elizabeth as she stepped from the boat with her delicate husband and her shy, sensitive, child hugging a doll.

The Filicchis were the first to welcome them, along with Carlton. "Come, Elizabeth dear. Our carriage is waiting. You don't know how happy we are to see you." She held out her hand. "Your troubles are at an end now."

"My dear fellow," said Antonio Filicchi, shaking hands heartily with William.

The crowd made a path for them to pass, and they were soon in the carriage. Some of the onlookers were from the Filicchi bank, and the counting house. Many were plain citizens who had come out of curiosity to see the Americans.

"*O, poverino!*" cried a farmer driving his oxcart. It was an expression of sympathy.

They drove through the great archway that led from Leghorn to Pisa. The ride from the waterfront to the boardinghouse which Amabilia Filicchi had selected for the Setons was a distance of fifteen miles.

There were so many new things for Annina to look at that she soon got over her disappointment that the Filicchi children had not come. Wide-eyed, she took in all the sights.

Antonio said to William, "You mustn't give a single thought to your future. All we want is to get you well again. Remember, you are to draw upon me at the bank for whatever you want."

Elizabeth's heart was so full it seemed to be brimming over. Now that they were free, gaiety took over. She talked of the fun they would have telling their experiences to everyone they knew in New York.

William and Elizabeth, when they reached the boardinghouse, were exhausted from the long drive and all the excitement. But no cricket could be livelier than Annina. She plied Mrs. Filicchi with questions.

"Who lives in those beautiful houses we passed on the way?"

It was explained to her. "Those palaces were

built by the grand dukes of Tuscany centuries ago. Their descendants live there now."

"And those gardens with the pretty fountains. Were they made long ago, too?"

"Yes, dear," said Amabilia, "long, long ago."

This was a fairy-tale world to Annina.

How heavenly it was to get a night's sleep. Peace! No sentry outside. No pounding waves. Only the Angelus bell to remind everyone of prayer.

After three days of rest and nourishment, William felt so much better that he wanted to go for a drive. The doctor whom Antonio had sent to attend the patient said, "No."

Like many sick people, William wanted his own way. He told the physician that if he didn't get some air he would suffocate. Fearing that arguments might be worse than exciting the patient, the doctor gave in.

The Setons set out in a carriage, but the exertion was too much. They were back again in no time. It was William's last ride.

Christmas Day dawned. Church bells rang out joyously to celebrate the birth of the Holy Babe. The landlady had decorated the house with festoons of leaves and bright flowers. Delicious odors rose from the kitchen.

Annina was happy. Uncle Carlton had given her a new dress. The carved figures and animals of the Nativity scene which the Filicchis had sent fascinated her.

Elizabeth thought of her children at home. Would they be together on Christmas Day? In whose house? Her heart ached for the joy of holding them close.

William was propped up in bed. "I wonder if it's cold in New York tonight," she said when the day was over. The North Dutch Church and the Old Coffee House on the Battery, would they be under a blanket of snow?

She saw the sadness in William's thin face. He turned to the wall to hide his tears. "I know I shall never see them again—Richard, nor William, nor . . ." He couldn't finish the sentence.

Elizabeth tried to comfort him, kissing him gently and smoothing his pillows. But when Carlton came to visit next afternoon he found an Anglican minister sitting beside the bed and Captain O'Brien at the foot of it.

William was dying. Hearing of it, the Filicchis had sent the minister, but William himself had asked for the captain of the *Shepherdess*.

"Promise me," William gasped, "that you will take my dear wife and Annina . . . back . . . to New York . . . on your return voyage."

Elizabeth heard the captain give his word. She marveled that her beloved William could speak of his own death with such resignation, without a shadow of fear.

Two days later William died in Elizabeth's arms. He was buried in the Protestant cemetery at Leghorn.

Every possible kindness was extended to the heartbroken young widow and her little girl. Amabilia called in a carriage every day to take the Setons for a drive around the countryside. Elizabeth wanted only to be alone in her sorrow, but she couldn't be ungrateful. Besides, there was Annina to think of. Poor little thing, she had cried so much over her father's death.

They visited the old cathedral in Pisa, the baptistry, and the Leaning Tower. Mrs. Filicchi bought a small model of the tower carved in ivory and gave it to Annina.

"You are a little puss," teased her mother. "You'll be quite spoiled by the time Amabilia has done with you!"

Annina chatted gaily about the flower gardens that bordered the river Arno. "Look, Mama!" She pointed to an old monastery. "Look at that old castle. It's falling to pieces. Will it come tumbling down the hill?"

At night Elizabeth wept in her loneliness, but during the day she thanked God that she had brought Annina with her.

"The *Shepherdess* will be sailing back within

another week," said Amabilia, "and you haven't seen one quarter of our beautiful buildings. We mustn't waste a single minute."

On the following Sunday Antonio and Amabilia came to ask if they could drive Elizabeth to morning service at St. George's Anglican church. But she surprised them by saying she would like to attend Mass with them. She felt she should, out of courtesy.

"We would be very happy if you'd care to come," they said with no little surprise.

Although at first nothing was very distinct in the church—it was lighted only by wax candles—Elizabeth's eyes soon became accustomed to the semidarkness. She saw hundreds of people kneeling.

The music of the organ was soft and distant. The lofty ceiling was of carved gold, the dome beautified with paintings. It was not the magnificence of the church that held her, though, but the solemn devotion of everyone present.

Young and old bowed their heads in prayer—some fashionable, some poor. Now there was a great hush. The priest was on the altar.

Elizabeth watched his movements, understanding none of them, but she found herself caught up in a kind of reverence she had never before experienced.

A gentleman of fashion knelt before a smaller

altar in an alcove. Next to him stood a poor woman whose shawl held a sleeping baby. Once again she was watching the priest, and Elizabeth felt a great longing to understand the meaning of the Mass.

When it was ended, she walked out with the Filicchis over the ancient mosaic that beautified the aisles.

Nothing was said of her first attendance at Mass. Neither the Filicchis nor Elizabeth wanted to discuss it. The fact that she had decided to go with them of her own accord was enough.

On the next day Elizabeth and Annina gave up their room at the boardinghouse and went to live with the Filicchis. What a magnificent home! It was called Castel Filicchi, and indeed it was a castle in Leghorn. There were a hundred rooms.

Built of stone and embellished with turrets in the medieval style, it overlooked the Arno River. What a contrast! From the miseries of the Lazaretto to a castle.

Annina skipped about in great delight, fancying herself to be a princess. Elizabeth was glad to see that the child was getting over her unhappiness.

"Now, you little puss, where are you?"

"I'm here!" Annina would say, popping up suddenly from behind a sofa.

The Castel traced its history back to the fourteenth century. There were rooms and rooms full of beauty. Some of the pictures and furniture reminded Elizabeth of the Seton home at Stone Street. It did not occur to her that her simple black widow's dress and bonnet must look strange in such magnificent surroundings. She was aware only that everything she had on was a gift from Amabilia.

With the great wealth of this kind family came a deep humility. The poor of Leghorn blessed them. They lived a saintly life. Mrs. Filicchi's heart was a fountain of goodness.

The entire household, including dozens of servants, attended five o'clock Mass daily. During Lent and on other days of penance, the family fasted until three o'clock in the afternoon.

Elizabeth, living in such religious surroundings, began to ask questions. She was convinced that what this family believed, they *lived*.

Driving one day to the ancient city of Florence, she and Amabilia, along with Annina, visited several of the famous churches.

On the way Elizabeth inquired about the Franciscan monks she saw walking the streets in brown habit and feet in sandals. How cheerful they were when anyone stopped and spoke to them.

The wayside shrines, decorated with dewy-fresh flowers, appealed to her sense of the beautiful. Elizabeth wanted to know about them.

The art galleries delighted her until her feet grew tired. Annina was full of questions. "Mama, why are there so many paintings of ladies called Madonnas . . . all of them different?"

Elizabeth smiled. "There is only one Madonna, darling. But each artist has painted her as he imagined her to be."

Elizabeth, turning homeward, wanted to visit the famous church of the Annunciation, in spite of her tiredness.

"We may be just in time for benediction," Amabilia said.

The huge church was almost filled although it was afternoon. Mrs. Filicchi led Elizabeth and Annina to chairs where they could see what was going on.

Benediction had just begun. The joyousness of the music, and the lovely Italian voices, brought tears to Elizabeth's eyes. Later, the gleaming golden monstrance in the priest's hands was lifted for veneration. Under a sudden impulse, Elizabeth prayed that she might accept the will of God . . . wherever it might lead her.

Then, out of the great stillness of the church, came the words of the priest: "Blessed be God."

The people answered. Their responses sounded like a faraway roll of surf on the shore.

When the last candle was put out on the altar,

there were only a few worshippers left. Amabilia asked Elizabeth if she wanted to go now.

After all the weeping she had done in her loneliness, Elizabeth was aware of a strange joy filling her soul. She couldn't have explained it, but it was there.

"Before we go, I'd like to look in the chapels at some of the famous mosaics I've read about," she said. But inside she knew it was an excuse to stay a little longer in the church that had affected her so deeply.

Feeling self-conscious, she dropped on her knees beside Mrs. Filicchi as they came to the Chapel of Our Lady. She prayed earnestly for guidance. Her path seemed strewn with uncertainty.

Annina looked up at the statue of the beautiful Madonna. "See, Mama," she whispered, "the lady is watching me. Do you think she's lonely up there?"

"Maybe she wants you to love her," Elizabeth whispered back.

When they reached the Castel Filicchi, Amabilia suggested that their children's governess should put Annina to bed. "You look so tired, Elizabeth."

She *was* feeling dreadfully tired, but she wanted to talk to Annina before the child climbed up into her big hand-decorated bed. Elizabeth gently refused the offer.

"Annina," she said after hearing her prayers, "did you feel that God was near you today in that church, listening to you?"

"Yes, Mama." Her eyes were serious.

"My little Annina," Elizabeth said, holding her close, "promise me you will love God always. No matter what may happen?"

She knelt upright in her bed and caught her mother's hands. "I promise."

"It is to love God that we are in the world. I've always taught you that, haven't I?"

Annina nodded solemnly. "Mama, will we go to the Catholic church when we go home to America?"

"I was wondering the same thing, but I don't know where there is one." She was thinking, would I have the courage to go there, even if there were?

"We'll talk about it in the morning, my precious." She stared down into the dark eyes and smiled.

"Good night, Mama."

"Good night."

The next day Elizabeth began to read books about the saints—about their poverty, their wisdom. New and beautiful thoughts were being planted in her soul.

The grief that had been so recent seemed somehow to take on a different meaning. This voyage in search of health for William, which had ended so tragically . . . was it the dark mountain of her strange dream?

This mysterious grace that was germinating in her soul . . . was it the green field on the other side of the hill?

Chapter Seven

THE FLAMINGO SAILS

EARLY in February of 1804 Elizabeth and Annina were driving down to the docks in Leghorn. The *Shepherdess* awaited their arrival.

What memories came before her as Elizabeth caught sight of the trim sails! How hopefully they had boarded her only a few months before. So much had happened since then.

The Filicchis wanted them to stay in Italy, but Elizabeth could not bear to be parted any longer from her four little ones at home.

A warm welcome awaited the two travelers

aboard the sailing ship. Remembering the promise made to Mr. Seton on his deathbed, Captain and Mrs. O'Brien had filled Elizabeth's cabin with flowers. "We couldn't do enough!" they said. "Your dear husband," the captain went on, "we admired him so much. . ."

Elizabeth wished he would say no more. It was hard enough to bid farewell to Antonio and Amabilia and to Annina's small companions. The thought of never again seeing William's grave was almost too much for her. Knowing this, she had begged her hostess not to see her off.

The afternoon was cold and blustery. She began to wish she had accepted the warm cape Mrs. Filicchi had offered. But the ship soon cast off her hawsers, and slowly began to glide away from the wharf.

Loneliness engulfed her. She wept from sheer exhaustion. Not one full night of sleep had come to her in weeks. It was now Annina's turn to worry.

"You look so white, Mama. You don't eat anything!"

She made a great effort to pull herself together. Already the ship was beginning to sway. There was fright in Annina's eyes. The child had not forgotten the Atlantic storms.

Watching from the deck, it appeared as if the ship were still and the scenery moving. In her tired state of mind, Elizabeth fancied that the spires of the churches were reaching out to her, entreating her to come back.

She was beginning to love Italy. The castles, the ancient ruins, the olive groves, the lemon trees, and most of all the faith of her people. If all her children were with her, she thought, she would never leave. But God had other plans.

No sooner was the *Shepherdess* headed out to sea than Annina complained she didn't feel well. "There's something wrong with my chest, Mama."

Elizabeth opened the buttons that fastened the back of Annina's dress and pulled part of it down over her shoulders. Her chest was covered with a bright red rash.

"Is your throat sore, darling?"

Her mother was frantic. Had the child got something contagious? Whatever was she going to do?

The ship began to roll alarmingly. The wind shrieked, and the sailors began yelling to one another. A hand came pounding at the Setons' cabin door.

"Mrs. Seton! Mrs. Seton!"

"Yes?"

Captain O'Brien shouted, "The ship's tossing like a shuttlecock! We're going to turn to. 'Tis better to return to port than to be missing altogether."

Sitting beside the feverish child while the tramp of seaboots thundered above them, Elizabeth closed her eyes in despair.

Then she began to think of the Chapel of Our Lady in the Florentine church. There she had received comfort. Why not pray now as she had then?

She repeated the words first uttered by St. Bernard in the Middle Ages. "Oh, Mary! Be our Mother!"

That cry of hers was the first Catholic prayer she had uttered. She felt a little frightened. Then she remembered that, having lost her own mother when she was not much more than an infant, she could find consolation in a heavenly Mother.

When the ship put into Leghorn again, the quarantine doctor looked at Annina and examined her chest. He pursed his lips and shook his head. "It's God's blessing," he said, "that the storm came up and the *Shepherdess* had to return. Your little girl has scarlet fever!"

Once again they found themselves back at the Castel Filicchi. Elizabeth's feeling of mortification was soon set at ease by her loving friends.

For three weeks she stayed in Annina's room, not allowing anyone to enter for fear of carrying contagion to the other children. When the child grew better, the doctor gave Elizabeth permission to write letters. The first one was to her favorite sister-in-law, Rebecca.

> "Oh, the patience and more than human kindness that these devoted friends have bestowed upon us. . ."

Three more weeks passed before she and Annina could set sail for home. To add to their troubles, Elizabeth herself came down with scarlet fever.

Later she was to see the hand of God in this, for it was during the long days of recovery that she read books about the Catholic Church and studied the lives and works of the saints seeking their pathway to heaven. She was fascinated by those whose vocation was to live in the desert or in a monastery in order to spend their lives in prayer, making reparation for their own sins and for those of the world. Elizabeth became absorbed in her spiritual discoveries.

Antonio Filicchi had long before decided to go to America in April. His passage was booked on the *Flamingo*. Important business would take him to Boston and to the big banking houses in New York.

It was Amabilia's own suggestion that Antonio should accompany Elizabeth and Annina on their return journey. What goodness of heart!

"The captain of the *Flamingo* doesn't have a good reputation," Amabilia said. "There may not be another vessel leaving port in weeks. Pirate attacks are still a grave danger on the high seas. It wouldn't do for a young and beautiful widow to travel without someone to protect her."

Elizabeth, knowing how heartbreaking it was for the Filicchis to be separated, could scarcely believe her ears. Yet, here was Amabilia offering her husband's protection.

"Are you coming with us, Uncle Antonio?" Annina asked, grinning at the prospect.

For answer, he stood rigidly at attention, saluted smartly, and, putting on a British accent he said, "Aye, aye, m' merry lass."

Annina giggled with delight. She adored him.

Cannon boomed from the deck of the *Flamingo* as a warning to the passengers that sailing time was approaching. She was a much larger ship than the *Shepherdess*.

A great hubbub was going on at the Castel Filicchi. When the hour came for parting with her husband, Amabilia burst into tears.

"I'll say good-by here," she sobbed. "I'll wave from the balcony as the ship goes by."

As a farewell gift, Filipo, Antonio's brother, gave Elizabeth a parchment scroll. It was a beautifully illuminated document.

"I've had this specially inscribed for you," he said. "I've heard about your interest in the Church.

This is a summary of the Catholic faith. It was prepared for you by a priest friend of mine."

"Filipo translated it into English himself," Antonio said with pride.

Elizabeth thanked him with all her heart.

"During the long voyage Antonio will explain any difficulties you may have," said Filipo.

"Those fifty-six days or more won't seem so endless," Elizabeth said, "now that I have this to study."

Carlton came at the very last minute. He was puffing. "Couldn't find a carriage when I wanted one. Had to run!" He lifted Annina up and swung her around until she laughingly begged him to stop.

"Please give this letter to Mama," Carlton said to Elizabeth. "It is to tell her that I've decided to study medicine. I'll be back to see her in Staten Island before too long. Tell her to write to me."

Soon the *Flamingo* was outward bound. Elizabeth, seated on the quarter-deck, thought of William lying beneath the green grass. "Farewell, my love," she whispered. "Your soul is in that great immensity where I cannot find you. Farewell."

So occupied was she with new spiritual thoughts that the long voyage did not seem so endless as she had expected. There were times when she felt her soul was at the breaking-point, for she knew what she would have to face in New York—the scorn of her best friends, opposition on all sides. How was she going to tell them of the new faith that was slowly, but surely, drawing her?

Coming into New York harbor, Elizabeth felt a lifting of the heart. It was good to see the old wharf again, and the warehouses. People were still leaning over the railings of the Battery watching the ships coming into port. From all parts of the world they came.

Greatest of all was the indescribable happiness of seeing her darlings again. William's sisters, Rebecca, Harriet, and Cecilia, would be on the dock to greet her. She strained her eyes in the hope of distinguishing them among the crowd gathered to welcome the *Flamingo*, but she was in for a disappointment. None of the Setons was there. What could have happened?

Antonio, as soon as the ship docked, said goodby to her. "Be assured of my continuous prayers," he told her. Then he left for Boston. There was nothing else for Elizabeth to do but take a carriage and drive home to State Street.

Hannah welcomed her with tears of joy. "The children are waiting in the nursery, ma'am. They're that excited I couldn't do anything with them!" Then she told Elizabeth the news. "Poor Miss Rebecca Seton . . . she's near to death, ma'am. That's why no one came to meet you."

Elizabeth felt her cheeks grow white.

"Now let me make you a cup of tea," said Hannah. "I've something special for Miss Annina. My, you both look so thin. I can almost see through you."

Shrieks of delight rang through the house. Elizabeth hurried upstairs to the nursery, her heart beating like a wild bird in a cage.

They crowded round the door. "She's coming! Mama's here!" It was Richard's voice. "Let's all rush out and hug her!" They were hopping up and down and clapping their hands.

"My darlings! My very own darlings!" She gathered them to her convulsively, showering them with kisses. I'm now both mother and father to them, she thought.

William eyed her solemnly. "Why do you wear that black dress? It makes you look different."

Kitty tried to stop his questioning. She was just old enough to understand why her mother was in mourning. "Mama will soon be wearing her pretty bonnets again. Won't you, Mama?"

"Not for quite a while," sighed her mother, who was hugging little Bec to her, spreading her fingers through the dark curls.

Annina kept them open-mouthed with stories of her adventures.

As soon as she'd had a cup of tea, Elizabeth hurried over to Stone Street. What was she going to find? A great welcome awaited her, but through their smiles she could see their alarm over Rebecca.

She was holding on to the last thread of life. When she saw her beloved Elizabeth, she smiled. "I'm very weak," she whispered, "but I did so want to live to see you. With you near me . . . I'm not afraid."

Their reunion was not to last long. Rebecca died two days later. When the family gathered to mourn Rebecca, Elizabeth spoke briefly to the Reverend Mr. Hobart, who conducted the service. He was looking forward to a nice long chat with her very soon, he said.

Now, a few days later, he was coming. How was she going to be brave enough to tell him what was in her mind?

He was waiting for her in the drawing room. During the voyage, she had gone over this scene in her mind so many times. Now it was here. Had he not been her spiritual adviser until now? He would be severe, his arguments eloquent.

Outwardly composed, Elizabeth trembled within. Courage! she told herself. She knew that he would take as a personal affront her earnest desire to be received into the Roman Catholic Church. She prayed for courage that she might not quail before him. If heaven were with her, she could face the rebuffs.

"Dear Mr. Hobart," she began gently, "how nice of you to come."

They talked of William, of the voyage, of Italy. And then: "Mr. Hobart . . ."

The learned clergyman looked at her, struck by her intense expression. "What is it?"

"I have decided to enter the Roman Catholic Church."

His face grew stern, his voice cold. "My dear child," he said, "don't you really think this . . . sudden . . . change is emotional? You've been through so much. And your friends in Italy have been so kind . . . you feel you owe them . . . something?"

His disapproval was sincere—and expected. It had not been easy for her to tell the minister, who was a friend not only to the Seton family, but to the Bayleys.

It was over now. She had stood firm. But what kind of future faced her?

Later she sat alone in her bedroom, an untasted supper before her. Hannah had brought it on a tray. "Unless you eat something," she had insisted, looking anxiously at her mistress, "you'll never get strong. You pray more than you eat, ma'am."

"Hannah, you've been such a faithful friend," Elizabeth said. "I don't know why you stay. I see little chance of ever paying you."

"Oh, ma'am," returned the girl, "I wouldn't leave you and the children for anything."

Elizabeth had eaten nothing when Hannah returned for the tray. Her lamp burned late into the night. Her fingers beat restlessly on the table. There were still a few things she could sell. Her mind flew to the diamond locket William had given her. It would be like parting with her heart's blood, but it must go.

Only one thing she would never dispose of— William's beautiful Stradivarius. That must be kept for one of the boys. She couldn't bear to think of anyone else's playing it.

How was she going to support her children? Could she teach, perhaps? Her father had told her long ago that a friend of his was leaving a large sum of money in her will to Elizabeth. At least she could count upon that one day to pay for the education of the boys. But what of her three girls?

The Seton family had helped a little. But they, too, had lost most of their money and were selling their country home to meet their own expenses.

Somehow news of Elizabeth's decision to enter the Church had reached Charlotte. She came in haste one afternoon.

"What is this I hear?" she demanded. "Is it true? I can't believe it. What will our friends . . . what will everyone . . . ?" She was too agitated to finish her sentence.

"Dear Mama," Elizabeth said, "I'm sorry to upset you. But I beg of you to try to understand. I firmly believe the step I'm taking is the right one."

Anxiety was in her face as she spoke. "If our ways lie in different directions, please don't let us be bad friends."

But Charlotte rose to take leave. "I'm utterly shocked that you should think of betraying your father's church and mine." Indignation was in her voice, and the plume in her bonnet trembled.

"But Mama. . ."

"I'm glad your father didn't live to see this outrage," she broke in, making her way towards the door. "All I can do is pray." She swept from the room and let herself out of the front door into the waiting carriage.

Mrs. Seton's strange behavior became the chief topic of conversation over many New York dinner tables.

"How could she leave fashionable Trinity Church to go to St. Peter's where the immigrants congregate?" people asked one another.

Elizabeth and Annina were watched going to early Mass. When she was scolded for this, she had an answer.

"Those people who go to St. Peter's are sometimes shabby and often hungry, but they wouldn't think of beginning their day's work without first attending the Holy Sacrifice. Does that seem wrong to you?" She spoke gently always. When she found her indignation rising, she turned away to swallow her anger before she answered.

Her inner conflict became an agony. It was like the pendulum of a clock swinging to and fro. I must . . . I mustn't . . . I must . . . I mustn't.

Every morning she made up her mind to present herself at St. Peter's rectory for instructions. Every night she had failed to do so. What was causing her timidity now?

It was her children. If she became a Catholic, they, too, would face scorn and ridicule. Could she subject them to these things?

A letter from Antonio Filicchi, expressing hope that nothing would deter her from fulfilling her great desire, sent her marching to St. Peter's. There in the rectory she declared her intention of becoming a member of the Catholic Church and began her instructions.

Returning to State Street with a light heart, she found a letter waiting for her on the hall table. The writing was unfamiliar. She unfolded it and read:

"Dear Mrs. Seton:
    As you may already know, I had made out a will leaving you a certain sum of money. Word has reached me that you are thinking of becoming a Catholic. In the event that you do, you will not receive one cent. . ."

Suddenly she felt very tired. What am I to do? she thought. All her hopes for the education of the boys hung upon that legacy. She sat down at her desk and wrote two letters—one to Antonio, the other to Amabilia. "Soon I'm going to be received," she told them, and asked for their earnest prayers.

Now she felt better. Taking off her bonnet, she crossed over to the window. Scraps of the children's talk reached her ears.

"What d'you want it for?" Kitty asked.

"For something."

Kitty persisted. "I'm not going to give you my crayons until you tell me what they're for."

A little later Annina shyly sidled up to her mother at the table. "Mama, I've made you something."

"What is it, darling?"

Annina handed her a drawing made with crayons. "Know what it is, Mama?"

Her mother's smile widened. "Of course I know. And it's very good. It's a drawing of the good ship *Flamingo*."

Chapter Eight

DECISION AT ST. PETER'S

In the face of criticism from every quarter, Elizabeth went daily to St. Peter's Church in Barclay Street for instruction.

The hours she spent studying under Father Matthew O'Brien were the first happy ones she had known in a long time.

"If you only knew the pitiable situation to which my poor soul had been reduced," she told him one day, "finding no satisfaction or consolation in anything but in tears and prayers."

Father O'Brien nodded. He understood thoroughly. "You will need courage to face all those who will turn against you," he said. "But in you, my dear child, I see someone who is not afraid, for you have heard and obeyed a divine summons."

Elizabeth wrote to Antonio about her instructions. Soon he replied that the most fitting place for her to be received was in Baltimore. "The church there is so beautiful," he went on, "and Bishop John Carroll should be the one to officiate."

"Not for all the world," she told him, "would I be so ungracious to dear, patient Father O'Brien."

The magnificent Church of the Annunciation in Florence was dear to her heart, but now St. Peter's, with its inspiring painting of the Crucifixion over the altar, was more precious to her.

When Harriet and Cecilia came to visit her, she told them once, "When I look over the rooftops from State Street and see that cross on the top of St. Peter's, I send up a little prayer."

"You've actually got roses in your cheeks again, Betty," Cecilia commented. "All your troubles seem to have vanished when you come back from your instructions."

Cecilia had a love for things spiritual. Both she and Harriet had something to tell their sister-in-law. "Do you know what we've been reading, Betty?"

Elizabeth slipped her arm around Cecilia's slim waist and looked into the lovely, oval face with its soft delicate coloring. "No, what have you been reading?"

"A Roman Missal!"

"Yes," Harriet added smiling, "and every time we do, I look up at the portrait of Papa—you know, the one Gilbert Stuart painted—and feel sure he is scolding us for reading it."

"You're heaping trouble on your own heads, my darlings," Elizabeth warned them, "but I'll take the blame if anything is said—and it will be!"

March 14, 1805, was the day of Elizabeth's reception into the Church. Antonio Filicchi acted as sponsor and witness and presented her formally to Father O'Brien at St. Peter's. All the dreadful months of indecision were over. They fell like a cloak at her feet.

Late that night she wrote to Amabilia: "In preparing for confession tomorrow, there is no great difficulty for me. Truly my life has been spent in bitterness of soul these past months."

Before leaving on his return voyage to Leghorn, Elizabeth presented Antonio with a copy of the *Imitation of Christ*. On the flyleaf she inscribed the words:

"Antonio Filicchi, from his dear sister and friend, Elizabeth A. Seton, to commemorate the happy day he presented her to the Church of God."

The children, seeing her so happy, asked how she felt now that she had become a Catholic.

"My darlings," she said, "I feel like St. Peter when his chains fell at the touch of the divine messenger."

On March 25 she made her first Holy Communion.

Now that there was no longer any chance of changing her decision, tests of Elizabeth's courage came from all quarters. Old friends pitied her, others taunted. Even the shopkeepers who had once valued her patronage hesitated to serve her. She was hurt deeply. What a terrible situation! In those hours she wavered between hope and grief.

She must look for somewhere to live. Perhaps a boardinghouse. Every dollar must be stretched as far as possible. There was no one to help her except the Filicchis. She knew that so long as her health lasted, her spirit would never fail. Work must be found somewhere.

What deep roots 8 State Street had grown in her heart. Now that she had to part with it, she remembered what she had written in *Dear Remembrances* the day they had moved in to their first house: "My own home at twenty! The world and heaven, too. Quite impossible!"

Then something unexpected happened. Hannah had answered the door to a knock. A strange man and woman stood on the doorstone. They gave their names as Mr. and Mrs. White.

"Could we speak to Mrs. Seton?" the man asked. "It's important."

"Well . . . I'll see, sir," Hannah said. "Will you please come in and wait in the hall?"

She described the callers. "They seem very nice, ma'am. The gentleman has an English accent. I think they're friendly."

After Elizabeth had greeted them in the drawing room, they explained the object of their call.

Mr. White began. "My wife and I are about to open a school for boys and girls on the Bowery near St. Mark's Church. You doubtless know where that is."

"Oh, yes." Elizabeth began to wonder if they were hoping to include her children among their pupils.

Mr. White coughed, looked around at the large room, now almost bare of furniture, and went on.

"We have heard of your desire to obtain a . . . a . . . position." He stopped, gave a short, dry cough, and looked around. His face expressed his thoughts. Why is a lady who lives in a house like this looking for a position?

Mrs. White took up where her husband left off. "We would like you to teach in our school, Mrs. Seton. You are a lady of education and travel, and you . . ."

"But I must tell you," Elizabeth interposed, "that I may not be proficient in the subjects you wish taught. I'm not at all skilled."

"If you will accept our offer," Mrs. White went on, "we shall consider ourselves fortunate."

They were soon discussing salary and duties.

Elizabeth smiled at the end of the interview. "I wondered who you could possibly be when you came this afternoon, but now I know you are my good angels."

She invited them to stay for coffee, then introduced her children. The salary offered was small, but part of the bargain was that Richard and William, Kitty and Annina should be educated at the Whites' school.

"What charming children," Mrs. White said when they came into the room. William, growing tall, had bright gold hair and a proud way of holding himself. Richard, just the opposite, was dark, and with a flash of roguery in his brown eyes. Annina curtsied, followed by Kitty, who clasped the eager hand of Bec.

Watching them lovingly as they moved about the room, Elizabeth almost forgot that she was being interviewed and that a new door had been opened to her.

With a grateful heart she thanked Mr. and Mrs. White for their kind offer and for their faith in her. "You'll find me most anxious to learn," she said.

"We know that you are accomplished and that you love children. We couldn't ask for more," Mr. White assured her.

How strange it seemed, a few weeks later, to be taking her children to school early in the morning. Bec wanted to go and didn't like being told by Kitty that she was only a baby.

Elizabeth found a great joy in knowing she was supporting herself and her family. She couldn't help thinking how astonished William would have been to see such a thing.

Even with her salary, she couldn't have provided the children with neat clothes and shoes, and still have money for food, had it not been for the kindness of the Filicchis and of Julia in Philadelphia.

She accepted the gifts of money in the spirit in which they were given, not feeling mortified, nor being in a state of wounded pride. She was thankful to God for the wonderful friends He had given her.

When 8 State Street passed into other hands, the Setons moved into a rooming house at the corner of Broadway and Fourth Street. The noise of passing coaches and wagons kept Elizabeth awake. At the end of the street a pump handle that squeaked and groaned horribly every time someone came to draw water was a source of great annoyance. But she would get used to it!

One morning news came from Philadelphia that Julia, who had been a widow for some time, had now lost her little daughter. She begged Elizabeth to come and visit her. "I'm completely alone," she wrote, "and cannot bear it."

Immediately Elizabeth made inquiries. It would take two and a half days to get to Philadelphia. A stage boat left from the pier in New York for South Amboy. Then a wagon would have to be taken from Burlington and still another before she could reach Julia. It was out of the question. She wrote a letter of explanation.

When Elizabeth was taking up the hem of one of Annina's dresses so that Kitty could wear it, a messenger came with Julia's reply.

"Since you cannot come, Betty darling, and I am so aware of your financial difficulties, I would like to provide for Annina the things I would have given my own child. . ."

Her eyes filled with tears. Dear, kind Julia, she thought. With her own heart breaking, she thinks of us.

That night Annina and Kitty were working at their lessons. When their mother came into the room, Annina ran to her, hid her face in the full, black skirt, and sobbed.

"Darling, what is it?"

"Oh, Mama . . . Mama," she cried, "don't send me to Philadelphia. I want to stay here with you."

Elizabeth embraced her impulsively. "And so you shall, my darling." They walked together back to the table. "Aunt Julia only wants you to go and stay with her for a while. You see, she's lonely. But, come now, no more tears. There are lessons to be done."

It wouldn't do anyway, Elizabeth thought sensibly. The child is used to poor circumstances now. It would be disturbing to live with riches and then come back home to so little.

Still only thirty-one years old, Elizabeth's beauty was enhanced by spiritual happiness. She began to feel that the future was assured. Poor health was her only worry. So long as she could go to early Mass every day at St. Peter's and continue with her teaching, all would be well.

William, nine years old, grew more like his father every day. A real boy, nothing delighted him more than stories of the sea. The life of a sailor was for him.

"Better study your math, then!" Elizabeth said, shaking a reproving finger at him. "Men of the sea must know foreign languages, too. Mr. White said your French exercises weren't good this week."

She smiled to herself. I sound like Charlotte scolding me for not practicing my harpsichord.

Beginning to really enjoy teaching, Elizabeth felt that her dreams for the children's future might be possible. Her hopes were soon to be dashed, for the school failed. If that was not bad enough, she was blamed for the disaster.

Gossips spread the rumor that she had taken the position of teacher at the Whites' school only so that she could advance her new religious ideas. Not one word of this was true. That she was teaching in order to earn bread for her children was the fact most overlooked. The failure was indeed due to the anti-Catholic feeling of the time, not because of Elizabeth alone, but because it was discovered that Mr. White was a Catholic himself.

For anyone else such a disaster would mean utter despair, but Elizabeth saw it as a test of her faith. Prayer was her source of strength. "Thou art my Father. Thou wilt place me above sorrow."

Now she was threatened in earnest. People who had positions in the government of New York began to persecute her. She received an official notice one day.

"The City of New York will be forced to remove you as a renegade if you continue to exert your influence on the minds of the young. . ."

She could read no more. To a person of her sensitive nature such false accusations were cruel. To be branded as a corrupter of little children was too horrible. Tears of anguish filled her eyes.

But Elizabeth was a woman of action. She thought of Canada. Perhaps dear Father O'Brien might suggest some employment she could find among Catholics there. She would speak to him after Mass in the morning.

She was prevented from doing this. A message came, brought hastily in a carriage by a maid from Stone Street. Something was wrong there.

"Hurry, Madam," said the maid. "Miss Cecilia is very ill. They need you."

The fact that she had been forbidden in the Seton house since her conversion didn't stop her. Cecilia wanted her; that was all that mattered. Putting on her bonnet and shawl, she got into the waiting carriage with the maid and drove off.

Cecilia was calling for her as the maid ushered Elizabeth into the sick girl's bedroom. No one else was there.

"Oh, Betty, darling," Cecilia cried out weakly, "they've been saying terrible things to me." She grabbed and clung to Elizabeth's hands as if afraid to let them go. "I'm so glad you came." She heaved a sigh which ended in a sob.

"What is it they're so angry about? How could they say cruel things to anyone so sweet?"

Cecilia struggled against her tears. "It's all because I told them that I'm going to become a Catholic. If I weren't so ill, they would have turned me out of the house. They said they'd send me away to the West Indies. Oh, Betty, only you and Harriet understand. But she is afraid to be on my side . . . she says . . ."

Elizabeth alone knew the fearful consequences that would follow if a child like Cecilia, only fourteen, should go against her family's wishes. "You must wait, darling, until you get well."

"They blame you," Cecilia began to sob again, "and I do love you so. They know I'm going to die . . . and so they let you come."

Elizabeth kissed the burning forehead and saw that she had soothed the child she loved as her own. "You're going to get better, and I'll stay with you until morning if you like."

In Cecilia she saw a courage far beyond her years. The little patient spent a restful night and was much better in the morning.

What changes! What changes! Elizabeth thought as she passed by the darkened ballroom where she and William once danced. Now every door in the house was closed against her as she went down the wide staircase and out into the street. She had sent a message to the boardinghouse keeper to ask her to look after the children until the morning.

They welcomed her as if she'd been away a week. It was the first time she'd missed daily Mass since she became a Catholic. But breakfast had to be prepared for her family, even though she had scarcely had a wink of sleep all night.

"We'll all go to St. Peter's and pray for Cecilia's recovery," Elizabeth said, "and, Bec, you shall light a candle for her at Our Lady's altar."

Kitty was looking out of the window after breakfast. "Mama," she called out, "the boy who brings the mail is coming down the street. I wonder if he has a letter for us."

"Look, he's coming here," said William, hurrying to the door and returning in triumph. "There's one for you, Mama."

Elizabeth scrutinized the letter. "I don't recognize the handwriting." When she unfolded it, the letter proved to be of great importance. It was an offer to teach at another school.

Chapter Nine

THE TOWN WHISPERED

ONE Wednesday night in July, 1807, Elizabeth was startled by a rap on the door of her room. She had just tucked the last child into bed and was about to retire herself. Who in the world would come at this hour?

She heard a carriage drive away. "Someone to see you," said the landlady in a voice which showed her displeasure at having to get out of bed.

"Cecilia!" Elizabeth exclaimed as she opened her door, "what has happened?" She hugged the frightened fourteen-year-old girl to her.

Once inside Cecilia let her bundle of clothes fall on the floor and flopped into a chair. She looked so white that Elizabeth thought she was going to faint.

"I've come to stay with you, Betty," the girl said as Elizabeth removed her flowered bonnet and took her Paisley shawl.

"But, the family? What will they do?"

Cecilia burst into tears. "They've turned me out," she sobbed. "I was received into the Church yesterday at St. Peter's. I was afraid to tell them until tonight. They've forbidden me to go back . . . ever."

Elizabeth kissed her softly. "God has specially blessed you for your brave spirit," she said, "and you knew you would be welcomed here." She also realized that this was a serious situation. It must be handled carefully. How could a family be so cruel, she thought, to a child whom God had, so recently, given back to them?

"Tomorrow you must write a letter to them," Elizabeth said, "asking them to take you back. Tell them you will obey them in everything but the renunciation of the Catholic Church."

"But, Betty, I did. I told them that." She stopped to blow her nose. "It made them angrier than ever!"

"When the storm blows over they'll send for you," insisted Elizabeth. "Now, dear, I'll make you a cup of tea. Tomorrow, when I come back from teaching, we'll talk this all over."

For quite a while Elizabeth had been working for Mr. Harris in his school. Now he suggested that she open a boarding school for his boys. This she did. Annina and Cecilia helped as well as they could. But for the consolation she received at Mass, and in her constant prayers, Elizabeth knew she could never cope with the task before her. The care of a household of unruly boys wore her out. Her health began to suffer.

As Elizabeth had expected, Cecilia's conversion had caused the town to start rumors afresh. Her life became a daily martyrdom. As she and her young sister-in-law went to do their marketing, they met with open snubs. The whispers grew and grew until life became impossible for them.

Annina had made her first Holy Communion. William and Richard would soon be making theirs. Elizabeth was surprised to receive several letters from as far away as Boston, praising her for taking in Cecilia and for the example she was setting be-before those who sought to destroy her reputation. In these she found courage for further battles that were bound to come.

More than once Cecilia showed signs of distress at being rudely spoken to, but Elizabeth calmed her. "One day we'll look upon these insults with gratitude. Bearing things calmly is the beginning of perfection." Then, seeing the perplexed little face, Elizabeth would laugh and say, "Heaven forgive you for making me preach. I'm only beginning to learn myself!"

Harriet visited them in secret. "I came to warn you of trouble that's coming," she said. "I hear about it wherever I go. What are you going to do?" She was a picture of dejection.

"Harriet, dear," Elizabeth replied, "so long as the children are not harmed, we'll face it."

Late next afternoon, when Elizabeth was having supper with her children and Cecilia, two well-dressed women came to the front door and pulled the bell.

Cecilia spoke to them and asked them to please wait a moment.

"They look like trouble, Elizabeth," she said quietly. "They want to see you and won't take no for an answer."

Elizabeth swallowed hard. Here it comes, she thought.

Squaring her shoulders, she put on her imaginary armor and said, "Ask them to come in."

"Shall I take the children into the bedroom?" Cecilia asked.

There was no time to answer. The two women had come in and stood blocking the doorway.

"We're in the middle of supper," Elizabeth explained. "I hope you won't mind."

"No need for the children to hurry," said the first woman. "Let them finish eating. We can wait."

The children's eyes, round and frightened, stared at the strangers. "Finish quickly," Elizabeth said, "and Cecilia will put you to bed." Then, turning to the women, she drew forward two chairs for them.

"We came at this hour purposely," one of them began, "because we wanted to be sure of your being at home." Open warfare was in her eyes.

The second woman opened her mouth to speak, but what she was about to say was cut short by her friend.

"Mrs. Seton—and this applies to your sister-in-law, also—we've put up with enough of your fanatical ideas in this town. What you do with your own soul is your affair. But when you use your influence upon others . . . little innocent children in school . . ."

Elizabeth felt cold from head to foot. She could hardly keep from shaking. But she would face their accusations calmly.

"Madam," she said, "you do me great injury. Not one word of religion has passed my lips to the children placed under my care by Mr. Harris."

The woman drew a gasping breath. "We expected you to deny it. But we are not falling under the spell of your supposed innocence, as others have done." She glanced in Cecilia's direction, and her lip curled in derision. "We have influence here, and you have been warned before. You chose to ignore our warning. Now, we order you to . . ."

Rising, Elizabeth faced the women squarely. "Please wait until the children have left the room!"

Cecilia, taking her cue, herded the frightened girls out of the door and closed it behind her.

"Now, ladies," Elizabeth said with outer calm, "I shall leave New York as soon as I find means of earning bread for my children. But this I repeat. There's not a word of truth in your accusations— not one word!"

"We'll be the judges of that, Mrs. Seton," said the woman, rising and giving a nod to her friend to indicate the interview was nearly over. "If you attempt to do any more teaching, the boys will be forbidden to enter the classroom."

By the time the two women had let themselves out of the front door, Elizabeth was shaking so that she had to sit down before she fainted. Never had the future looked darker.

"I pray so much," she said to Cecilia a few days later, "that when I awake, my mind seems to have been praying."

But now things were happening fast. She received a letter from Amabilia offering her a permanent home with them in Italy, but she wanted to remain in America. William and Richard were at school at Georgetown College, at Washington, D.C., where their tuition was being paid by Antonio Filicchi. She would not dream of deserting them to go to Leghorn. I will face the future in my native land, she thought.

She gave up the boys' boardinghouse and went back to the rooming house where she had lived before. One day, after receiving Holy Communion at St. Peter's, she went into the rectory to ask Father O'Brien's advice as to her future.

A distinguished priest and educator, Father Du Bourg, had said Mass at her beloved church that morning and was in conversation with the rector when Elizabeth entered.

"Father Du Bourg," said the Irish priest, introducing her, "this is Mrs. Seton, the widow of whom we have just been speaking."

"I heard a great deal about you," said Father Du Bourg, "before I came to New York. You're a courageous woman."

In her black dress and somewhat rusty bonnet, Elizabeth felt anything but brave. "Thank you, Father," she said, "but I confess I came here solely for help and advice. I never needed it more."

Father Du Bourg looked at her gravely. "I think you may be the one to help *me*," he said.

Elizabeth didn't hide her astonishment.

"For many years," Father Du Bourg went on, "I've been aware of the necessity for a school in

Baltimore. You've had experience with teaching, Father O'Brien tells me. There is no Catholic school for girls there. I believe that you would be the very person to run it."

Was this the answer to her prayers?

One of the few friends left to Elizabeth was a Mrs. Barry. Was it a coincidence, or was it by the grace of God, that she had promised to take coffee at Mrs. Barry's house that afternoon? When she walked in, who should rise from his chair to greet her but Father Louis Du Bourg!

"Isn't this the work of Providence?" he asked, smiling. "I had no idea Mrs. Barry knew you until I mentioned your name just now."

Naturally they talked of the subject nearest to the priest's heart. "At the moment we have neither the money nor the school, but a house could be rented if I could persuade you to come to Baltimore."

Elizabeth felt her cheeks reddening. "Don't think me ungrateful, Father. I'm just a little overwhelmed."

"Such a big question requires a great deal of thought," he replied. "Perhaps you will write to me after I return to St. Mary's Seminary in Baltimore."

When she returned to her rooms, she couldn't wait to tell Cecilia. "Just as everything seemed darkest, a new light shines," she said, taking off her gloves and bonnet. "We get discouraged so easily. Why don't we leave things in God's hands?"

She wrote to Bishop Carroll in Baltimore, asking his advice. He, in turn, discussed the matter with Father Du Bourg. It was settled.

"Come to us, Mrs. Seton. Here in your work you will find great consolations. Courage is not wanting in you and, as for your dear children, they can be very happy here, too."

Early on a beautiful June morning in 1808 a procession of Setons left the boardinghouse on Fourth Street for the last time. It was the beginning of a great adventure for Kitty and Bec—their first journey on a packet. Annina was familiar with sailing ships.

That morning Elizabeth had stood on the corner of the street opposite St. Peter's, taking her last look at the church. She gazed at the gray stone building, winking back the tears. Never would she forget the square tower ending in a bell-shaped cupola.

On the top a golden cross gleamed. How often, from her window, she had seen it shining over the trees and the roof tops.

One traveling basket was all the Setons carried between them. A week before Elizabeth had forwarded, by another boat, the old trunk—a relic of the voyages back and forth across the Atlantic.

"Better bring a few necessities," Father Du

Bourg had suggested. "You won't be able to get much here."

There were no fears in Elizabeth's mind now. Bishop Carroll and the friends of Antonio had agreed to this plan. All she had to do was to have faith, accept her new responsibilities, and leave the rest to God. Fourteen-year-old Cecilia was happy staying with friends.

"I feel like Columbus," said Kitty when the boat began to swing around. Six-year-old Bec clapped her hands in delight. "Where are we going, Mama?"

"To the mysterious South where none of us has been before."

"Not even you, Mama?"

"Not even I."

Annina, now thirteen and as tall as her mother, was silent. She seemed wrapped in deep reverie. Her delicate look caught at Elizabeth's heart. *She realizes that this is a decisive moment in her life— in all our lives!*

Kitty and Bec could hardly wait to get there.

I'm now an exile, thought Elizabeth, *just like those poor immigrants I used to pity as a child. But I have a new life to go to, new friends to make.*

"Mama, how green and beautiful the sea is. And the seagulls—how gay they are, circling and circling over us." Kitty had never had such an exciting day. Elizabeth was looking at the receding skyline, breaking with the past, turning her back upon the city of her birth forever.

A glorious morning welcomed them when they touched the soil of Maryland for the first time. A wagon met them, sent by Father Du Bourg. The sun was marching across the sky by the time they reached St. Mary's Seminary.

A ceremony was in progress when they reached the chapel. Solemn High Mass was being celebrated. The altar, bright with flowers and candles, was thinly veiled in incense.

"Mama, something very special is going on, isn't it?" Kitty whispered as the Kyrie of the solemn Mass burst forth. Priests and seminarians sang together.

"Yes. It's a special day for the seminary," she whispered back, "the consecration of their new chapel."

Kneeling with her children, Elizabeth humbly dedicated her life to God.

"Look, Mama," Bec said softly, "the sun's shining right through the pretty windows on you."

When the ceremonies of consecration were over, they waited outside for Father Du Bourg.

"How long do we have to wait?" Bec asked ten minutes later.

"She's hungry!" Kitty was voicing her own feelings.

They were received with great kindness by the

priests at St. Mary's Seminary, of whom Father Du Bourg was the superior. A meal was served which they had by themselves in the guest parlor.

"It's nicer inside than it is outside," Annina remarked. "It looks like a prison, or the Lazaretto!"

When they had finished their meal, Father Du Bourg came for them.

"My mother and sister are expecting you," he said. "You will enjoy staying with them, I hope."

"How kind. But aren't there too many of us?"

Mrs. Du Bourg's house was not far from the seminary, set in the midst of shady trees.

"This is a very happy occasion for us, Mrs. Seton," said Mrs. Du Bourg in the friendliest manner. She gave Elizabeth a motherly kiss on both cheeks. "And the dear children! Welcome, welcome to all."

Annina carried the traveling basket upstairs to the large room prepared for them. A familiar sight greeted her eyes—the old trunk that had been sent on ahead. She touched it happily as if it were an old friend.

"You're not afraid of us, are you?" said Father Du Bourg's sister coaxingly to Bec who was too shy to speak.

When the lamps were lighted and the children asleep, the three women talked. Outside in the darkness horses clopped along over the cobblestones every now and then. Mrs. Du Bourg's face was gentle and tranquil, but she loved to chatter.

"Dear, dear Mrs. Seton," said the old lady, after she had talked for almost half an hour, "you look a little spent. I shouldn't have said so much."

Elizabeth was indeed dead tired. It had been a long journey. I almost went to sleep, she told herself in consternation, while Mrs. Du Bourg was speaking.

A breeze stirred the curtains, and a smell of jasmine came in through the window.

"Let me take you to your room," said the old lady, rising and crossing the parlor to the stairs.

"Thank you so much," Elizabeth said, following her until they reached the landing.

The bedroom door was open. The light from the oil lamp reflected upon the three sleeping children. Her heart contracted with love for them. What was to be their future?

Somewhere in the trees a mocking bird sang.

Chapter Ten

NO MONEY IN THEIR POCKETS

WITH their usual generosity, the Filicchis not only approved of the idea of the school in Baltimore but made arrangements to supply the money —at least enough for the initial expenses.

When Elizabeth left New York she carried $1,000 of Antonio's money. This she gave to Father Du Bourg.

"Here is a beginning, Father," Elizabeth said, feeling a new strength lifting her up. She saw in the priest's eyes a great happiness. His years of patience were being rewarded.

Within two weeks a two-story house on Paca Street had been rented, and the Setons moved in.

"This is fun," Kitty said when the old trunk was opened. She wanted to pull everything out.

Elizabeth restrained her. "There's one thing I want." She bent down and lifted a long thin object, carefully wrapped in a shawl.

"What is it?" Kitty wanted to know.

"It's your dear father's Stradivarius, the only thing of value I've kept." She touched the fiddle case with affection, then unlocked the snap. In a blue velvet lining lay the instrument. In the upper part was the bow. "This is for William. I promised it to him long ago."

Kitty stood looking at the violin. "I don't remember Father at all," she said.

"Nor do I," Bec remarked, pulling out of the trunk a red dress, "but I do remember this. It's my favorite."

Their words came as a shock to Elizabeth. She had forgotten how small they were at the time of William's death.

The rented house was nicely situated between two orchards, about two miles from the city. Only the barest necessities were bought. As soon as they were settled Elizabeth began working with her usual zest, happy that St. Mary's chapel was only a stone's throw from them.

The priests at St. Mary's were consulted—

Father Dubois, Father Flaget, Father Bruté and, of course, Father Du Bourg. Then announcements were sent out.

Elizabeth made out schedules for her classes. She considered what books must be obtained, and where. Annina set to work copying histories and French exercises in her neat longhand.

On the morning of the first day of school Elizabeth told Father Du Bourg that she couldn't help feeling a little frightened. "It's such a serious matter . . . this business of trying to lead others."

The French priest smiled. "You have courage, I know. Just think of this experience as a kind of novitiate, a preparation for the future."

"I'll try," she said, nervously tightening the strings of her bonnet.

"It's example we want," Father Du Bourg went on, "and in you we have it."

Grateful for his encouragement, she walked down the steps of St. Mary's chapel, across the lawn, and in through the gate in front of the house.

Kitty brought her a cup of tea, a scone, and a dab of damson preserve. "Mama, make haste. You'll have time to eat only a little bit. It's almost eight o'clock."

Annina was in the schoolroom puttering among the books, arranging the benches and the table to her satisfaction.

Noticing Kitty's laughing eyes, Elizabeth fingered the ringlets that hung loose on the child's neck. "This is a happy day for you, isn't it, sweetheart? You'll have new friends to play with."

Annina came into the kitchen at that moment. "Did she tell you what she was trying to do this morning?"

Elizabeth looked at Kitty askance. "Something terrible, was it?"

"No, Mama. I was only trying to climb on the back of the old gray horse in the orchard. He didn't mind. He only pricked up his ears and paid no attention."

Just then the front door bell clanged.

Next moment Annina was saying, "Good morning." She was greeting the first pupil.

He was eight years old. He wore long, tight-fitting white trousers, a blue jacket with brass buttons, and stood politely holding his hat.

Within a few months children were coming from all parts of the town. Some were brought in carriages from the old main road to Annapolis. Others walked two miles or more. At first it was going to be only a girls' school, but so many parents begged Elizabeth to take their sons that they changed their original idea. Perhaps the school for girls only would come later. Soon there was no room. The children that were brought from the old Philadelphia road had to be refused.

"What are we going to do about the *poor* children?" Elizabeth asked Father Du Bourg one day. "There are so many of them." They had been going over the school accounts.

"The way you've kept your books does you great credit, Mrs. Seton, and I think it won't be too long before we can afford to think about a free school. But where are we going to have it? And how are you going to make both ends meet?"

"Our cupboard is a little bare," Elizabeth said with a smile, "but we have plenty of faith."

Father Du Bourg's heart brimmed with happiness. "Our hopes in you, Mrs. Seton, were well founded," he said. "I believed you to be the one person who could head this work. Now you've proved it."

"Thank you, Father," Elizabeth said humbly. "But I won't be quite happy until I can teach the poor children. They're so sweet and trusting . . . I just love them."

"If we had an assured income, like the Sisters of Charity in France," said the priest, "then we could think seriously of a free school, but we must be patient."

"May I suggest something to you?" Elizabeth asked. "I've received quite a number of letters from women and young girls who would like to join me in this work. Would you consider my having help?"

Father Du Bourg's eyes opened wide. "If you

would let me show those letters to the bishop, perhaps something could be done!"

"I don't want to complain," Elizabeth said. "But
so many pupils keep me so busy that, really, if
someone doesn't give me a helping hand . . ."

"You shall have help," said Father Du Bourg
emphatically. Armed with the letters, he went on
his way, determined to gain an appointment with
the bishop.

Within a few weeks, permission being granted,
Elizabeth received several replies from those who
wished to give their lives to Catholic education.

Without really being aware of it, she had
formed a small community.

The house on Paca Street was not without
gaiety. Elizabeth's laugh was often heard. It was
one of her great charms. "Work gives glory to
God as much as prayer," she said once when she
and her helpers were scouring pots in the kitchen.
"I remember reading about St. Teresa of Avila.
She lived in the sixteenth century. 'The Lord
walks among the saucepans,' she wrote in her diary.
I've never forgotten it."

Mothers as well as children sought Mrs. Seton's
advice. In the town, the apothecary, the chandler,
the old woman who sold her milk, all greeted the
"frail little lady from New York" with respect and
affection.

The old Italian bookbinder always inquired if

she had any news from his country—"the land where the lemon trees bloom," as he called it.

Late one afternoon in May Father Du Bourg paid the budding community a visit. He settled himself in the chair Elizabeth offered and told her the object of his call.

"Our Holy Father, Pope Pius VII, some time ago was pleased to elevate Bishop Carroll to the title of archbishop. I've just come from seeing him. I wanted you to know immediately what he has planned for you. So pleased is he with your work that he wants to place you and your companions under proper religious status."

"You mean for us to become sisters?"

Elizabeth covered her face with her hands. "Oh, gracious!" she exclaimed, leaning forward and almost losing her composure. "We are none of us good enough for that, especially me. I'm sure I couldn't."

The priest smiled. He had expected that she would be overwhelmed. "What about obedience?" he said.

Elizabeth clasped her hands in her lap, not knowing how to answer him.

"I realize you are under no formal vow," he explained. "But I want you to think of it as a call to obedience. Your day would be almost the same as at present. You live, work, and pray in common. You benefit by the instructions at St. Mary's on the religious life. To belong to a sisterhood is a holy privilege."

Elizabeth, too overwhelmed to give her answer, promised to convey the archbishop's wishes to her companions.

On the feast of Corpus Christi, just a twelve-month after her arrival in Baltimore, Elizabeth and her devoted followers appeared at Mass in the habit of the new sisterhood.

It was a long black robe and short cape, much like the dress worn in Italy by widows. The head-dress of white crimped muslin had a tiny black band to hold the cap in place. It ended in a small black bow tied under the chin.

In the presence of Archbishop Carroll, Eliza-beth pronounced her religious vows, and the title of "Mother" was conferred upon her. From then on she was to be known as Mother Seton.

At her request, the new community was placed under the patronage of St. Joseph.

Now began the great work that was to start in the hills of Maryland and, carefully nourished, was to spread throughout America.

Mother Seton dreamed dreams, but her feet were firmly planted on the ground. She had disci-plined herself to face reality. Griefs of her own made her understanding. Memories of Revolution-ary War privations helped her to face poverty. Skilled in nursing, no sickness frightened her. And yet, with all these virtues, the greatest was humility. It required no little courage to be mother to a group of women whose goodness, she felt, far surpassed her own.

Already the community of St. Joseph was growing. The population of Baltimore had increased a hundredfold in the last ten years. Catholic children came crowding into the school.

"We must have a bigger building," Mother Seton told the priests at St. Mary's.

"You seem to get everything you pray for," Father Du Bourg said.

"But where is there some land for sale, even if we could get the money to buy it?"

"That, my child, is where you come in," the priest said. "Just double your prayers!"

Two weeks later Mother Seton went through the white gate and across the grass to St. Mary's. She asked for Father Du Bourg.

"Your smile tells me that you have good news," said the superior of the seminary, catching her excitement.

"I have a strange question to ask you, Father. Is there a Mr. Cooper in the parish, or amongst your students?"

Father Du Bourg's face lighted up. "There certainly is. He is about to study for the priesthood. Why?"

"If I were not so sure of this, I would hesitate

to tell you. It's something that cannot be explained." For a moment she hesitated. "This morning, after Communion, I distinctly heard a voice. The words of the message were, 'Go! Speak to Mr. Cooper. He will give you what is necessary for your establishment.' " Mother Seton stopped, feeling frightened, wondering now if perhaps she had imagined it.

Father Du Bourg pondered, trying to be calm in the face of this strange thing that had happened. "If it is God Who has spoken to you," he said, "He will make His will known to Mr. Cooper, too. We must wait. And, in the meantime . . . pray!"

Mother Seton prayed longer than ever before. It was almost morning before she flung herself on the bed, exhausted.

Next day Father Du Bourg called again at the house on Paca Street.

"I have something of great importance to tell you," he said, and there was a look of triumphant happiness on his face. "Last night, when the whole seminary was asleep, I was working at my desk. Mr. Samuel Sutherland Cooper came to me and offered a sum of money. 'I have been thinking,' he said, 'that nothing has been done for the education of Catholic girls. After all, they do grow up to be a great influence in the future of America.'

"I could scarcely believe my ears, Mrs. Seton," Father Du Bourg said.

Mother Seton felt her heart beating wildly. Then it was the voice of God! "Please go on," she said.

"Samuel Cooper placed on my desk a small packet. 'In there,' he told me, 'you will find bonds to the value of $10,000. They are yours. Build a school with them.'

"Then I told him about you and what you had heard. That voice . . . that message!

" 'Strange that I've been at St. Mary's all this time and yet it was only tonight that the thought about building a school came to me.' Those were his words."

Samuel Cooper and Mother Seton met for the first time that evening. They discussed the proposed school and its possible location, but nothing definite was settled.

"I would like to put the wheels in motion at once," the young seminarian said to Mother Seton. "But Father Du Bourg has refused to accept the money for a while. He wants me to have ample time to think it over."

"Somehow I don't think you'll change your mind," Mother Seton said with a smile.

"You are quite right. I never shall!"

Sitting at her writing table a week later, Mother Seton heard the sound of horses' hoofs on the cobblestones outside. She looked up. Was she having visitors?

It was a carriage. The driver pulled his horse to a stop. Two girls climbed down. They were coming in through the white gate.

Mother Seton opened the door. She caught her breath and flung out her arms to welcome Harriet and Cecilia. The man stood waiting with a trunk.

"Oh, Betty, darling!" They hugged her close.

"Bring the trunk inside and put it anywhere," Elizabeth said to the man. When he had gone and the door was closed, she asked, "What happened?"

"We've come to join you if you'll have us," Harriet answered.

"But what of the family?" Elizabeth asked, taking Harriet's hands in hers and reading trouble in her eyes.

"We've been disowned." Harriet explained. "They found out I'd been seeing Cecilia."

Elizabeth threw her arms around Harriet. "Now we're all together and can face anything." After some refreshment she told them of all the plans for the future.

A site had been found by Mr. Cooper.

"The house is at Emmitsburg, a village about forty miles from here. A beautiful spot in the shadow of the Blue Ridge Mountains," he enthused. "I'm so happy about this, Mother Seton."

She smiled. How well she understood.

"It's not quite ready," he said, "but my friend, Father Dubois, has recently founded a new seminary near there and has placed a small log house at your disposal. You and your companions are welcome to stay there until the house is ready."

This was wonderful news. Mother Seton could already imagine all those little children, rich and poor, streaming across the fields with their catechisms and their writing books. . .

Mr. Cooper had another message to deliver. "Father Dubois told me to warn you that the log house has its discomforts. I think he said some of the windows don't have any glass."

Mother Seton laughed. "We'll manage."

On June 21, 1809, they set out—a small band of women and children, followed by a covered wagon containing their few possessions. They had nothing in their pockets, but a whole world of hope in their hearts.

Chapter Eleven

THE STONE HOUSE

So that Mother Seton could be near her two sons, now twelve and ten years old, she arranged with the professors at Georgetown College in Washington, D.C., to transfer William and Richard to the newly opened mountain-top seminary near the new convent.

It was towards this place that Mother Seton and her companions made their way. Maria Murphy, who had recently joined them, and Harriet withstood the fifty-mile-journey well, but Cecilia found it too much. She rested as well as she could on a mattress, laid flat between sacks of potatoes on the bottom of the covered wagon.

The horses drawing the battered old vehicle had to be walked more than half the way. The wagon creaked and groaned, lurching from side to side. The loose pots and pans rattled against each other as it jolted over the dried ruts in the cowpaths.

All their worldly possessions went with them— an old clock, several chairs, a tea caddy containing some of the precious cured leaves to be used on feast days, candles and home-made soap, one oil lamp, two lanterns, three mattresses, some linen, and a few table utensils.

Besides the potatoes, there were two sacks of turnips, three loaves of coarse bread, dried meat, and peas.

Carefully wrapped in a thin blanket were two precious statues, one of Our Lady and one of St. Vincent de Paul, founder of the Daughters of Charity in France in 1633.

Leading the horses through the tangled under-growth, Mother Seton thought regretfully of the little boy who had stood crying outside the gate on Paca Street. He was one of her pupils. He had seemed heartbroken at being left.

They had figured that the journey would take them roughly three days. At midday the sound of woodchopping could be heard and the rattling of pewter plates.

Mother Seton was preparing food. Annina and Harriet clattered along with a bucket of water which they had drawn from a spring. In no time at all the dried wood was flaming. Meat, beans, and bread were doled out. Bec protested at having to eat such dried-up meat, but Mother Seton soon put that right. "You don't hear Cecilia or Harriet complaining, do you?"

Bec pointed to Kitty's plate. "She's not eating hers!"

Kitty began at once to demolish the food in question.

"Not one scrap of food must be wasted," Mother Seton said. "We're very poor," she reminded her children, "and must be very grateful for everything we have."

At night they slept on the ground, a lighted lantern near them. A blanket for each was the only protection against dampness. When the first streak of dawn appeared in the sky Mother Seton was walking among the trees, reading the prayers of her Office aloud.

When they came to a little settlement the farm people greeted them kindly, but with curiosity. It was unusual for women to travel across the lonely wastes without manly protection. Never before had they seen women wearing long black robes and white crimped headdresses.

The water reached up to the hub of the wheels

when they forded streams. Once they had to wait for the waters to recede so that they could cross a river.

On the second afternoon, while Cecilia rested and Harriet and Annina dipped the plates in a stream, Mother Seton and Maria Murphy read and meditated. Their thoughts turned to the work ahead of them.

"Where did Kitty and Bec go?" Harriet said, returning with the clean plates. Annina carried the cooking pot and the knives and forks. "I'll go hunt them. They can't be far away, the scamps!"

She found them in a thicket. They were sitting on the ground, their arms around their drawn-up knees, waiting for a rabbit to come out of its hole.

Sometimes in Paca Street Mother Seton had felt as if she had no bones to support her. But now she was filled with renewed vigor. Her head and heart were filled with the future. With faith, discipline and courage, she told herself, she could face any desperate emergencies that might arise. In the happiness of her vocation there was no time for past griefs.

"We shall reach the seminary in the morning," she said, stroking Kitty's hair, "and I shall see my dear boys again." She sighed happily. "I wonder if they've changed much."

"We'll have to tell them about the dear little rabbit," Bec said to Kitty. She opened her candid gray eyes. "I wonder if they'll go skating with me when the ice comes."

"That's a nice thought," said Harriet, who was finding the Maryland summer heat unbearable.

As their covered wagon moved ahead the next morning, they saw a black speck against the horizon. Gradually it took shape against the blue scudding skies and baked fields. They saw that it was a black-robed figure awaiting their coming. "It must be Father Dubois or one of the priests from the seminary. Thank God we've all got here safely."

Kitty and Bec laughed heartily to see their mother leading the horses and shooing the geese out of their path as the birds stretched their necks to see what the procession was all about.

The priest with a boy on either side of him now stood on the steps of the seminary at the top of the hill. Next moment William and Richard were tearing down the pathway, running like young deer. Shouting and breathing hard, they flung themselves into their mother's arms. The whole Seton family was in a state of wild excitement.

Kneeling together in the seminary chapel a while later, a Te Deum of joy was sent up to heaven—thanksgiving for a daring journey safely accomplished.

That evening Father Dubois escorted Mother Seton and Maria Murphy to the log house. It was much further down the hill. Maria did most of the talking, for Mother Seton was going over in her mind bits of the children's recent chatter.

Richard, after looking at Annina in admiration, had said, "She looks like the Madonna that hangs on the wall of the refectory at Georgetown College. She's quite grown up!"

William, admiring the Stradivarius, had touched it with reverence. "I'll take the greatest care of it because it belonged to Papa. One day perhaps I'll play as well as he did."

"Yes, Mama, I still want to go to sea." Richard was emphatic. "A sea boy whistling in the maintop shrouds. That's my sort!"

"I'm going to work for Uncle Antonio," William had informed her. "He says I can work at the Filicchi bank. I'll send you money for the school later on."

Bless his heart, she thought. He has ideas already of being a gentleman! A gentleman without a penny to his name.

Suddenly a voice broke into her thoughts. "I hope he warned you, Mother Seton." She realized with shame that Father Dubois was addressing her and that she hadn't heard him.

"I beg your pardon, Father Dubois?"

"I was just hoping that Father Du Bourg had told you of the inconveniences of this log house.

It's very primitive. But the Stone House won't be ready for some months."

What he had said about the log house was indeed true, but there was no word of complaint. With a few personal things about the place, they soon began to feel the little dwelling was home.

Mother Seton held as rigidly as possible to the set of rules the archbishop had given them in Baltimore. However, more women would have to join them before it could officially be considered a sisterhood.

In dreams she saw numerous young women, journeying everywhere, teaching the poor, teaching the children how to serve God, visiting the sick, especially the Negroes. When she awoke, she would pray earnestly that He Who had begun this work would one day bring it to perfection.

She loved to look out of the window in the attic at the misty Blue Ridge Mountains and the sweeping valleys. Watching the white clouds reminded her of the days at New Rochelle. At Uncle William's she had loved to watch the skies and wonder if her mother were looking down on her. Dipping into the future, she envisioned what Bishop Cheverus of Boston had once said to her: "I see choirs of young girls following you to the altar. I see your holy order diffusing itself in different parts of the United States . . ."

But what was she doing? Dreaming when there was so much to do! She hurried downstairs.

Sometimes, when their privations threatened to dampen their spirits, Mother Seton was the one to encourage those less heroic than herself. The stone house which Mr. Cooper was giving them still was not ready. It was not easy to be patient.

Letters came from Pennsylvania and surrounding Maryland counties from those who wished to join the community. Sadly, Mother Seton had to refuse. "We have no room at present. But I beg of you not to give up hope . . ."

The temporary altar which they had fixed up in the community room was never without wild flowers. Kitty and Bec gathered plants and rooted them in a patch they called "our garden."

Annina worked with her mother on textbooks, writing new ones and patching up the old ones. A wide correspondence had to be answered. Bishops and priests sought Mother Seton's advice on matters of education.

If she were not too tired, *Dear Remembrances* would have another page added. Putting down her thoughts eased the tensions of the day.

At last! At last! The Stone House was ready. It was July 31, the feast of St. Ignatius. Now they had a chapel of their own. It was what they wanted most of all. One of the priests from St. Mary's celebrated their first Mass.

The happiness of possessing the Blessed Sacrament made them forget the inconveniences of their everyday life. The chapel was only six feet square and partitioned off from the rest of the house by folding doors.

Soon the school opened. When the children came, Mother Seton's heart was so full of happiness she felt that another drop of it would spill over.

Annina and Cecilia, seeing Mother Seton's joy, talked of one day entering the sisterhood themselves, but Harriet felt differently.

"I'm doing my religious duties by helping with the teaching and doing the cooking," she said gently. "I feel my work is just as pleasing to God, even if I don't take vows."

"And so it is," said Mother Seton, who had just come into the room.

Letters still came from girls who wished to join the community.

"But we've scarcely enough food now," protested practical Harriet.

Mother Seton gave her a gentle reprimand. "We mustn't refuse anyone who earnestly wants to help us. It will mean eating a little less, but we'll manage somehow."

Harriet laughed. "We'll all be completely invisible soon!"

One day Mother Seton said to Harriet, "I'm thinking of sending Annina to Philadelphia. My dearest friend, Julia Scott, has invited her so many times. I think she ought to go."

"It would be good for her. She'd meet plenty of boys and girls of her own age. She should see a little of the world before she decides she wants the religious life.

"She seemed willing to go when I mentioned it. Last time it was suggested she couldn't bear the thought of being away. She's sixteen now, old enough to make her own choice." Mother Seton laughed. "You, and Annina, and Cecilia are so close in ages, and so devoted to one another, that sometimes I feel all of you are my daughters."

"How wise you are in everything," Harriet said. "And Annina! She's such a sweet, loving girl, not happy unless she's doing something for others. I've never heard her complain. She's a real little saint."

One of Aunt Julia's maids came for Annina. It had taken over three days to get there. Kitty and Bec made up a small bouquet and handed it to their sister when the driver took his seat.

"I wish you were coming with me," Annina said as she bade good-by to her mother, and to Kit, and to Bec. The whole community stood at the door of the Stone House and waved.

"Stay! Stay!" Kitty begged.

"Think what fun it will be when she comes back," said Mother Seton. But there were tears in her eyes. It was her first parting from Annina. She was going to miss her. Work was the cure for that.

Prayers, lessons, catechism, French, history, and sewing. Once a week Negro children came to the Stone House for instructions. At first they were so shy and embarrassed that she found herself saving milk and apples from her own sparse meals. With these she coaxed them.

Now they would dart across the schoolroom, catch her hand and pull at her skirts. Their large brown eyes looked up at her with love and confidence.

Harriet, who had never peeled a potato until she came to Baltimore, cooked for the household. She soon learned to make a meal from almost nothing. They were having the hardest struggle to make both ends meet financially.

As winter approached, further sacrifices were added to each day's privations. A few rough boards nailed across the attic windows were all they had to keep the snow from blustering in. Sometimes the wind whirled madly through the wide cracks, blowing out the candle as the sisters were going to bed.

On Christmas Day of the first year at Emmitsburg, they sat down to a meal of salt pork, buttermilk, and carrot coffee, made by drying the green tops until they were brown and boiling them.

Mother Seton wrote in her journal: "So earnest

was every heart at that table that their scanty fare seemed too good a living."

Annina wrote from Philadelphia that she was enjoying her stay.

"Aunt Julia has taken me to some gay parties. I've met lots of nice boys and girls. Tomorrow we go skating. The ice is thick. We go only on the fashionable upper lake. But, Mama, with all the excitement here, I never forget my religious duties . . ."

Mother Seton dearly loved her first-born. "I'm glad you give some time every day," she wrote, "to religious reading, darling. It is as necessary to the well-ordered mind as the hand of a gardener who prevents weeds from destroying your favorite flowers."

Winter was slowly merging into spring.

One day a mail coach pulled up outside the palings of the Stone House. Mother Seton watched from the small-paned window in the parlor. A woman descended, and the driver handed a bundle over to her. The man resumed his seat. Urging the horses, the coach swung on its dusty way down into the valley.

Who could she be? Mother Seton opened the door herself.

"I received your letter," said the girl, "and I've come to join you—that is, if you'll have me."

Mother Seton took the bundle from the new

postulant and told her how glad she was to see her. "Come along in." The door closed behind them.

"You must be hungry. I'll soon have something for you to eat. We have our meals in the kitchen. Follow me."

The newcomer's shoes made a clacking noise on the cobblestone floor.

"You'll have to put up with close quarters," said Mother Seton. "We have only four rooms here. The two large ones are given over to the school. But, with God's help, we'll grow!"

The superior and the postulant talked until it was candlelight time.

Rain fell for three consecutive days. It was a deluge. The roof began to leak. Water seeped down the attic walls. Harriet, so tired that she slept through the night under a water-soaked covering, became ill. Mother Seton, knowing only too well what dampness had done to the weak chests of the Seton family, became alarmed.

During the day, when she could be spared, Maria Murphy nursed Harriet. Mother Seton was giving lessons in the schoolroom, but her thoughts were upstairs with the patient. Later that night she found Harriet kneeling by the open window saying her Rosary. In September Harriet too had become a Catholic.

"Come, dear, you must go back to bed." She

helped her gently back onto the straw pallet and watched beside her until morning.

The young roundness of her face was gone. But a new spiritual light shone forth. The doctor, shaking his head, spoke to Mother Seton in the parlor.

"No one knows better than you, with your wide experience in nursing . . ."

"But she's only seventeen, doctor. Is there no hope?"

"None."

Mother Seton had to face the heartbreaking task of telling Cecilia what the doctor had said.

The fifteen-year-old girl caught her underlip with her teeth and ran out into the woods, sobbing.

Solomon wrote the words that have echoed through more than three thousand years:

"The winter is past, the rain is over and gone; the flowers appear on the earth; the time of pruning is come."

And so it was at the little community of St. Joseph's. In spring they were planting flowers on its first grave.

Beneath the poplars, in the clearing by the woods, Cecilia, with tear-stained face, knelt daily beside the newly turned mound of earth and prayed for the soul of her beloved sister.

It was Mother Seton, whose own heart had been torn by grief, who bade her not to be overcome.

"In the sanctuary Harriet loved so much, you will find consolation," she said kindly.

There was a sound of running feet across the grass. One of the school children had come seeking Cecilia.

"Oh, there you are!" said the little girl, then came to a sudden stop when she saw the familiar long black gown and the starched bonnet. "I didn't know you were here, Mother Seton."

"That's all right, dear. I'm going in now to prepare for our French lesson this afternoon. You stay a moment and talk to Cecilia."

When they were alone the child said, "Come . . . see what I've brought to school. It's for you. A big surprise."

Hand in hand, Cecilia and the child went and looked into a small basket which had been hidden behind the trunk of a tree. "There," said the small girl. "Look inside. It's for you."

Cecilia, smiling, found a black kitten curled up asleep.

Chapter Twelve

THE DREAM COMES TRUE

SITTING at the table in the parlor of the White House, Mother Seton talked to her religious family. They now numbered five. The newest ones were Mary Butler of Philadelphia, Susan Clossy of New York, and Elizabeth Boyle of Baltimore. Others awaited admission, but the White House was not yet ready for so many.

In February, 1810, Mother Seton had led the sisters in procession from the Stone House to the new White House Mr. Cooper had given them. But the White House was still far from complete.

Now it was August. A humid afternoon caused the flowers in the garden to wilt, but the listeners were quite unaware of discomfort. What Mother Seton was saying affected every one of them.

She had grown to love Elizabeth Boyle dearly. From the very first she had seen her as a wonderful worker, a kindred spirit, and a sharer in her burdens. It was always to Sister Elizabeth Boyle she went with her special worries. She, also, was a convert.

On the day before this talk which Mother Seton was giving, something had happened to cause a flurry of excitement at the White House. Bishop Flaget had traveled all the way from France to bring to the community a copy of the Rules of Saint Vincent de Paul.

"You all know," Mother Seton said, "how I have longed for us to follow his precepts. When the bishop brought them yesterday, I was almost overwhelmed." She smiled at Sister Maria Murphy. "It was while you were trying to scrape together a few cookies, and some of that precious tea in the kitchen, that the bishop gave the Rules to me."

Sister Maria smiled back. "If someone hadn't made a few little buns on Tuesday, we'd have been in a fine pickle!"

Mother Seton went on. "Some of you know about Saint Vincent. Even so, I would like to review his life—at least some of the high points—if only to refresh your memories.

"He was born in 1541 in France, the son of poor farmers. He used to say with humility that he was a swineherd. Later he showed a love for learning and began to study, hoping to be a priest one day. He traveled a great deal, meeting all kinds of people, some rich, some poor.

"Once, coming back by ship from Marseilles, he was captured by pirates and forced into slavery in North Africa. What he saw there filled him with such horror that he was determined to do what he could, if he were ever freed, for the wretched creatures he saw beaten, tortured, and starved to death."

Seeing her listeners' eyes bright with attention, Mother Seton went on. "Later, as you know, he did escape. He eventually took Holy Orders and chose to live among the poor.

"But he was equally well known, and greatly respected, at the court of France. Luckily he was appointed Royal Almoner of Galleys by King Louis XIII, but he continued to live in the slums."

Mother Seton could feel her color mounting as she told them the story. "Well, this was what he had waited for. Now, at last, he could help the wretched galley slaves. Remembering the horrors he had witnessed, he did all he could to alleviate their sufferings. Before long he had built a hospital."

No one in the little community room had stirred. The sisters were intent upon the saint's story.

"The unfailing love he had shown for all creatures made him known as Monsieur Vincent, the miracle man. He organized a society which he called the Daughters of Charity. These included some of the highest-born ladies of the land.

"Choosing to make great sacrifices for the love of God, these French women plunged into the cauldron of wickedness—the back streets of Paris. They entered disease-ridden tenements, embracing the sick as St. Francis of Assisi had done centuries before and staying to nurse them back to health."

Mother Seton paused, remembering what courage is required to do this. For a moment she forgot the sisters were waiting to hear more.

"Next St. Vincent turned his attention to the foundlings. Poor abandoned little souls! Paris was full of them, hungry, half naked, dying. Taking them in his arms, he gave them the first love they'd ever known. He built a foundling home."

"What a beautiful story," said Sister Elizabeth. "It's no wonder you want to follow his rules. But we'll never be able to do the things he did."

"Perhaps not. Not in our lifetime. But if we

prove ourselves worthy . . . there may be others who will follow us. We must leave all in God's hands."

The humidity was lifting. Now sunshine spilled across the room.

The crack-faced clock warned them it was nearing time for Compline, the religious exercise at the close of day.

"Tomorrow I shall send this copy of St. Vincent's Rules to the archbishop. I feel sure that, after making a few alterations suitable to American life, he will approve." Mother Seton nodded her head. "Until then we shall continue to follow the temporary ones he has set down for us."

Sister Elizabeth looked puzzled. "There's a question I'd like to ask. How are we going to subsist if we teach only the poor? We have no money. After all, there are only a few who are paying now."

"A good question." Mother Seton laughed a little helplessly. "Oh! there I go, rushing on again. I was so anxious to talk about Saint Vincent that I forgot to tell you the most important news. Here it is. The archbishop has given us permission to open a boarding school for young ladies when the white house is ready. In that way we can maintain ourselves."

"Oh, I see," Sister Elizabeth said. "Then after that will come the regular school for the poor."

Maria Murphy leaned forward. "But when do you think we'll begin?"

"It may take months," Mother Seton answered. "But, as Father Du Bourg says, 'Patience, my child. Trust in Providence.' "

"But they are taking so long to finish the house," protested Sister Maria. "Can't they be hurried?"

"It will come," Mother Seton said with finality.

Cecilia had once said, "I hope I can teach the littlest ones. They are so sweet."

But Cecilia did not live to see this hope fulfilled. Five months after the death of Harriet, a bed of earth covered Cecilia's grave. She was a child so sweet, so loving that her whole life had been passed in innocence.

"We must not weep," Mother Seton said to the nuns kneeling under the shadowy trees. "Our little Cecilia's life is only beginning. Her death is like the sunset of a beautiful spring day."

But in spite of what she said, her own voice was choked with tears. She wondered if she were to lose still more of those she loved best. Was suffering to be given her in full measure?

Autumn passed. Another winter came. The winds wailed and soon the trees were naked. Severe weather was predicted by the farmers. Milk froze in the pails. The earth became encrusted with frost.

Kitty and Bec, in the fall, had gone out gathering baskets of kindling. Crimson cheeked and irrepressible, they brought home twigs of scaly barked hickory and scrub oak, and broken pine branches. Now they burned in the fireplace, but the attic was bitter cold.

No complaint was ever heard. Once Mother Seton returned from the store in Emmitsburg and told the sisters it was impossible to get any more bombazine. "We'll just have to do a bit more patching. It's because of the war between England and America. The shopkeeper said later on he could get flannel, but pepper and salt color instead of black. Nice objects we shall look!" She laughed. "Well, penance is good for the soul."

Parents were writing from neighboring states, asking if their children could come to the school as boarders. The sisters were happy that people were getting to know about their work. "But they have no idea how small our quarters are," said Sister Maria.

"I shall write and beg the parents to be patient," Mother Seton said. "Two more letters came today. Will you add them to the list, Sister Elizabeth?"

The school was growing. In the summer weather, when the rooms were full, some of the children sat on benches on the porch for their lessons. But now that winter was here, they crowded around the log fire and didn't want to go home.

Sister Elizabeth Boyle and Mother Seton were strolling about the yard. "Look . . . they're starting on the dormer windows!" Sister Elizabeth's voice trembled with excitement. "This is a great day," she said to Mother Seton.

"It means the fulfillment of all our hopes and prayers." She clasped her roughened hands together and murmured, "Thanks be to God."

They were glad to go in and warm themselves by the fire after their walk. Annina was cutting out garments from some white material on the table. Kitty sewed neat buttonholes in a baby's jacket, the last item of a layette for a destitute family in Emmitsburg.

"How did you ever learn to cut things out with no pattern to guide you?" Kitty asked, watching her older sister with admiration.

Clip, clip, clip went the scissors. "At Aunt Julia's I learned a whole lot of things."

"How's the sewing coming along?" asked their mother.

"Soon be finished," Kitty said, proudly smoothing her work and admiring the tiny stitches. Then she looked up. "Are you feeling all right, Mama?" She noted the tired circles under her mother's eyes.

"Just a slight headache. It will soon go away. I've been writing too many letters, I expect, but they must be answered. People are so interested in our work. We cannot be grateful enough."

Next evening, after Compline, Annina went to her mother and said, "There's something I want to tell you, Mama."

It wasn't often they had a chance to talk together. "Sit down, dear, and open your heart. Is something troubling you?"

Annina began. "When I came back from Philadelphia and heard of dear Cecilia's death, I hadn't the heart to tell you. I was happy at first when I arrived there. All the kinds of parties you must have had when you were a girl! Oh, but after a while I was so homesick. All I wanted to do was to come back."

Mother Seton had realized how happy Annina was to come home, in spite of all the kindnesses showered on her.

"Mama, right in the middle of a merry party I realized that the gay, social life was not for me. There was never a moment to think."

"Julia meant to be kind," Mother Seton said reflectively. "She has no one to love. How we could use all that love here with our little ones."

"I've been thinking a long, long time about what I'm going to tell you. I wanted to be quite sure. Mama, I want to take holy vows."

Taking her oldest child in her arms, Mother

Seton said, "You've made a wise decision, darling. I don't think you'll find the robe of religion too hard to bear—no harder than life at the Lazaretto. Remember?"

"Give me your blessing as you used to when we were all little."

She signed the forehead of her kneeling daughter with a cross. "God bless you and safeguard your soul on its way to a holy life."

The last shingles were being hammered into place on the roof. Workmen cleaned up the debris. Wheelbarrows rolled over the newly made paths. Shutters at the windows gleamed with fresh paint. Mother Seton's dream had come true.

She heard her name called as she walked about near the new convent. It was one of the workmen. "I just wondered, Ma'am, if you had a rosary you could spare. Mine's broken in pieces."

"I couldn't refuse you anything," she said, smiling. "Come along and I'll give you a lovely one." The carpenter walked beside her. "Will the house be completed soon?" she asked.

"Sure as you're standing here. And God bless you and the good sisters for all you've done for us in Emmitsburg, Catholic or not!"

Later, Mother Seton turned to Sister Elizabeth with tears in her eyes. "I should be so happy, I know . . . but I'm frightened! Such a solemn undertaking—guiding little children, being responsible for their souls. Will I be able. . . ?"

Dear, understanding Sister Elizabeth reminded her of St. Vincent.

"He must have felt the same way when he first saw his hospital completed. He must have been scared, too, but he went forward. Are you not a daughter of St. Vincent?"

Mother Seton's misgivings were put to flight.

The free school opened first, as that part of the building was ready. The girls' school would follow.

"What a blessed day this is for everyone!" Father Du Bourg was speaking to the other Sulpician priests who had come with him. His smile was infectious. William and Richard walked around proudly, showing Father Dubois the house, as if their mother had built it herself.

One of the happiest people that day was Samuel Sutherland Cooper, who had been inspired to give his money to start this great work.

Before leaving, Father Du Bourg spoke to Mother Seton in the hallway of the White House. "It was prophetic that I should have met you at St. Peter's. This I do know. It was no chance meeting! In you I saw the one who could bring this project to reality. It was the will of God."

On the verge of tears, Mother Seton bowed her head. "You make me feel very humble. Pray for me, Father," she begged softly. "Pray for all of us."

"I will, my child. I will. You have fought courageously. But much more will be expected of you, for you have received a great grace."

From the depths of her soul she answered, "Pray that I may never refuse God anything."

Chapter Thirteen

EMMITSBURG AT TWILIGHT

OVER a hundred little girls were chanting their night prayers. In the shadows, the voice of a novice led them. Candles burned clear. Over all one thought . . . God is listening.

Outside the valleys of the Blue Ridge Mountains were painted pink with apple blossoms. The last ray of golden sun looked in through the windows. Slowly the light faded and the shadows lengthened. It was the spring of 1811.

Once the children were seen safely to bed, other voices rose in prayer. Seventeen sisters and novices, tired from the long day's duties, each in her own way was thankful for blessings. Soon night would fall gently over the slumbering White House. There was peace at Emmitsburg.

In her room Mother Seton lay awake in the gray silence, her eyes directed at the shadowy crucifix hanging on the wall. How it consoled her! Out of the past she was remembering the old French-woman who had clung onto the little gold one she always wore around her neck in those days. It had meant so much.

Now her own mind kept wandering to and fro, in great agitation, from one sickroom to the other. Isolated, in another part of the house, she had just left Annina. She had dropped asleep after a bad day of coughing and fever. Three weeks ago the delicate girl had been ordered to bed. There were no signs of improvement.

At Philadelphia Bec lay in a hospital, suffering from a broken hip and badly injured knee. Last winter she had gone skating, her cheeks as bright as the red coat and bonnet she wore. She had slipped and fallen. Her friends had carried her home, unaware of the seriousness of her accident, although her screams could be heard far away.

Only ten years old and she was crippled for life. Everything possible was being done. Julia came forward and offered to take Bec to a famous surgeon in Philadelphia.

Gratefully, but with a breaking heart, Mother Seton had sent the little invalid there—a distance of almost a hundred miles—in the care of a trusted friend.

For two weeks Mother Seton had waited in agonizing suspense. At last the letter came. Julia wrote to say it was hopeless. After a painful operation the surgeon had said Bec would never walk again.

She lay thinking of that letter now.

". . . the child talks so often of the grotto on the mountain where you and the sisters take the children for picnics on Sundays. I cannot bear to think that she will never again . . ."

"Sweet Bec," Mother Seton sighed. "Her heart is like a bright star at the bottom of a fountain."

Kitty was as healthy as the boys, but Annina had seemed so improved in health of late that the sudden illness had come as a shock. There was always hope. She would be better after a night's sleep.

"Please take some milk," Kitty urged next day as she sat beside her older sister. Her hand trembled as she held the cup. "Let me give you just a sip?"

"No," Annina said weakly.

There was a gentle rap on the door. Kitty opened it. Two of the boarders stood hesitantly.

They were not supposed to go into the isolated room. There was a fragrance around them.

"We've been picking lilies-of-the-valley," said one of the girls, bringing a bunch of them from behind her back. "They're for Annina."

Kitty took the flowers. "Oh, thank you. They're lovely. But I mustn't let you in. You can see her from where you are."

The girls looked thoughtfully at the quiet figure on the bed and went away on the verge of tears.

Once again the season for gathering grain was here. The flail resounded from the barn at the foot of the hill. Annina never rallied from her illness. She grew weaker until the flame of life flickered and went out.

She had asked so often to become a Sister of St. Joseph that, a few days before she died, and by special permission, she made her profession.

Annina was laid to rest beside her aunts, Harriet and Cecilia, amidst the silent tears of the school-children. Mother Seton's heart was stricken beyond grief.

Her beloved "bearer of burdens," Sister Elizabeth, sought to console her.

"I'd rather see my beloved Annina go," Mother Seton said, "than for her to stay and take my load of sorrow. I must suffer patiently. My winter will soon be over, and the spring that succeeds will blossom eternally."

The work had to go on. More and more American girls came to Emmitsburg, wanting to consecrate their lives to charity and to teaching. The community was growing. Not only those interested in education, but the poor and the ignorant, came to Mother Seton for advice. She listened with the utmost patience to everyone's problems.

"Mama, can't you rest a while?"

Kitty had come into her mother's room. The desk was piled high with correspondence and books. Some of them were open and turned face down. Others bristled with bookmarks.

"I will soon, sweet child," said her mother, looking into the inkwell. "When this is dry I'll stop. That's a bargain."

Kitty peered into the depths of the pot herself. "That's going to be pretty soon. It's almost empty now." She looked at her mother with troubled eyes. "You scare me when you work so hard. Please don't get sick."

Lovingly Mother Seton reached up and took the round chin in her hand. "Dear Catherine. I think you should no longer be called Kitty. You're growing up—almost twelve. You mustn't let trifles worry you."

"But Mama . . . what would I do . . . ?"

"Because I'm tired is no cause for alarm. I have many responsibilities. Money matters, bills to pay . . ."

"I know, Mama." Kitty picked up one of the leather volumes on the desk. "I know you have an awful lot to do, but there's no need to be translating French books into English, is there?"

"You know, I see in you a born manager." Her mother smiled. "I think you're going to be a great help to me soon." She looked at the pile of manuscripts she had written in her neat hand. "As for these translations, they are spiritual works. They don't exist in English, and we couldn't afford to buy them if they did."

Sister Maria stood in the doorway. "Sorry to disturb you, but that poor old Negro woman from the Morris' farm . . . she insists upon seeing you. No one else will do, she says."

The pen was thrust back into the inkpot. "I'll come."

Kitty tried again. "Mama, don't go. You're much too tired!"

"Catherine, my dear. A Sister of St. Joseph must never, never be too tired. Always remember that."

There were visits from the boys. How Mother Seton looked forward to the hour she spent with them on Sundays. Their chatter brightened up her ever-present anxiety over Bec. Questions were batted back and forth like shuttlecocks.

"How's the Latin this week? Doing better with math?"

Triumphantly Richard caught a fly that had

been buzzing around him. Then he let it go. "Father Dubois is such fun, Mama. He tells us funny stories right in the middle of a math problem!" Then, thumping his chest, "Do you know how much I've grown in six months, Mama? Over an inch. What do you think of that?"

William's eyes were serious. At fifteen he seemed such a man. "Mama," he said, "couldn't Uncle Carlton write to us from Italy and tell us who's the best surgeon in America for Bec?"

Mother Seton's eyes clouded with tears. "Aunt Julia wants to take her to Dr. Chatard's in Baltimore. He's a very clever man. But how can the poor little creature, unable to sit or to lie without great pain, possibly go on such a journey? My gay little Bec . . . never to walk again."

"But," William went on, "she's coming home first. After you've nursed her for a while she'll feel stronger. And it won't be as far as Philadelphia."

Just before Lent, two years later, Mother Seton sat at her desk, writing in a leather album. From the back cover a hinge lay flat beyond the edge. She was writing the last page of the *Dear Remembrances*.

She had said to herself, after Bec had died in her arms, that there must be no more grief for the past. Only the future . . . and action! Tears ran down her cheeks as she made the last entry in the book wherein she had poured forth her soul since childhood.

> "So pure the sky over the dear graves, Bec's already covered with greenest moss, and even a little violet in full flower on it. I look out of my window onto the woods where my darlings sleep . . . no more pain now . . ."

Slowly she closed the leather covers. Lifting the brass hinge, she fitted it into the corresponding clasp on the front and snapped it together. Then, taking a small key from a drawer in the desk, she turned it in the tiny lock on the book.

Opening the window, she threw the key as far as possible into the wooded thicket. I must think only of our work . . . of the plans God has for our future . . . of the little souls under my care, and theirs. Tomorrow, she thought, I'll hide this book where it will never be found.

All the sisters were a little sad at heart that the archbishop had taken so long to give his formal confirmation of their order. Three years of patient waiting had passed.

On July 19, 1813, the archbishop gave his sanction to the Rules of St. Vincent. At last it had come. The rejoicing was great. Now, truly, they were progressing.

A group of eighteen women, led by Mother Seton, now pronounced their vows of poverty, chastity, and obedience. The solemn ceremony officially constituted the religious order of the American Sisters of Charity.

A slight change in their former habit was made. The white crimped cap of the Paca Street beginnings was replaced by a black bonnet.

Such was her love for the little children who came as boarders that Mother Seton treated them as if they were her own.

One little girl of six had cried bitterly when her parents were leaving her. Knowing a mother's anxiety, Mother Seton wrote to them:

"Dear Mr. and Mrs. Delaware,

"Your little darling has passed through her trial of separation admirably. It is now the third day since you left her. She is sleeping soundly and eating well. Sweet child, she has such an affectionate heart, she has already come to love us . . ."

No matter how crowded her day, a letter to ease a parent's anxiety must not be put off.

The busy years passed rapidly. On his eighteenth birthday William was at sea, but he had managed to get a letter delivered to the White House the day before. It was November. Under the bare trees, and wrapped in a black shawl, the person who loved him best was reading it again and again.

"My beloved Mother:

"As you have asked me so often to do, I look up at the heavens in the night watch and pray for you. Could you see my heart, you would find nothing but your dear self and those who center in you . . ."

She stopped reading and pictured her boy, a midshipman in the United States Navy, waving to her from the deck of a great vessel. . . .

Then a bell rang in the crisp air, bringing her thoughts back to where she was. She bowed her head and said the Angelus.

For twelve years Mother Seton carried on her work. She saw the Sisters of Charity grow and grow. She opened two missions—a hospital in Philadelphia in 1814, and an orphanage in New York City in 1817.

A true American daughter of St. Vincent, her love for the poor and afflicted, the despised and the ignorant, was her silent way of serving her beloved Master, Who said: "Inasmuch as ye have done it unto one of the least of these My brethren, ye have done it unto Me."

Once, when she was very ill, she called Sister Elizabeth to her side.

"Will you write a letter for me?" she asked. "While I've been lying here I've been thinking how much God has done for us at Emmitsburg.

And yet . . . we have no fitting chapel." She smiled weakly. "Betsy, dear, I want you to write to the archbishop and ask his permission to build one."

"But how will you possibly raise the funds?" Sister Elizabeth asked.

"Oh, I know it sounds as if I'm out of my head. But write just the same."

"Of course, I will," said her most devoted co-worker, who had taken over the handling of the enormous expenses until Mother Seton was well enough to resume her work.

The chapel became Mother Seton's dream. Once again her prayers were answered. The archbishop granted his permission. To the great relief of everyone, she rallied from her illness. All those around her worked harder than ever.

In almost no time, it seemed, enough money had been gathered, in large and in small sums, to begin the building. Everyone joined in the fund raising. Contributions came from rich and poor. Never before had the frail superioress of St. Joseph's Convent been so happy.

One day a novice came to Mother Seton and said, "There's a lady in the parlor. She wishes to see you. She said, 'Just tell her I'm a very old friend of hers—someone she hasn't seen in many years.' She wouldn't give her name."

When Mother Seton walked into the parlor, her heart seemed to take a great leap. Sitting in the armchair was a woman dressed in rich velvet and furs. She ran to Mother Seton and kissed her on both cheeks. "Elizabeth!"

"Julia! Oh Julia, my dear! After all this time."

There were so many years to cover, so many things to say.

After a while a novice brought in tea.

"Tell me about William," Julia asked.

"He's on the ship *Macedonia*. It left for an unknown port some weeks ago. President Monroe appointed him a midshipman. He's just the same sweet boy he always was."

"And Richard?"

"He's in Italy. Doing well with the dear Filicchis. We could never pay back the debt of gratitude we owe to them . . . and to you."

"Now tell me about Catherine."

A proud smile crossed Mother Seton's face. "I see in her someone who will carry on this work long after me. She's so strong and capable. But dear Julia, what of yourself? I can hardly believe you are really here . . . after all the coaxing I've done."

Julia laid aside her muff and leaned towards Mother Seton. The years seemed to fall away. Once again it was as if they were sitting under the plum tree at Uncle William's in New Rochelle.

"Elizabeth, dear," said Julia, "I can't call you Mother Seton yet. I'm not used to it. I came for two reasons. You'll be surprised to hear I've become a Catholic at last. I've been years thinking about it. Well, now I am. And, as a sort of thanksgiving, I've brought you a thousand dollars. Use it for anything you like. Here it is."

From her bag she drew some papers. "It's all in bonds. You can put it to better use than I. Take them with my love."

Mother Seton looked astonished. "You knew nothing about the fund for the chapel?"

Julia shook her head. "No, nothing."

Silently Mother Seton gave thanks. She had so long hoped that the joys of her own conversion would be shared by the friend of her childhood. "This gift of money will help to build the chapel that is the dearest wish of my heart. God bless you, dear Julia."

Julia took the small hands that she had known only as white and soft. Now they were roughened by the thousand menial tasks that had needed to be done. "You've been so brave, Elizabeth, through the heart-breaking losses of your darling Annina, and little Bec . . . so wonderful. . . ."

Mother Seton's eyes shone with tears. But they were not from sadness alone. The trace of a faint smile flickered across her face.

"God took my little girls to Himself," she said softly. Then, as if seeing into the future, she added,

"But He has given me many many other daughters."

Once again it was twilight when Julia's carriage drove off down the hill. In the air was a solemn stillness. A small figure in a black habit and bonnet walked slowly to the old well under the trees.

Elizabeth Ann Seton was thinking of her childhood. Then she had sought the spirit of holiness in the woods, in the sea, in the sky. She had found it at Emmitsburg, in the little children, in the joy of serving, and in the Sisters of Charity.

———————

Today, from the four corners of America, and across the seas as far as the Indies, you can see the Sisters of Charity carrying on the work of Mother Seton.

From the Stone House in Emmitsburg, the American Catholic pioneer, Elizabeth Ann Seton, inspired others to follow her into the great fields of education, nursing, and the caring for orphans, the homeless, and the aged.

Now the Sisters of Charity maintain 150 hospitals, as well as sanitariums, foundling homes, Negro and Indian schools, and a refuge for lepers. More than 10,000 Sisters of Charity have learned from the story of Mother Seton's life—a model of perfection, an inspiration by which to carry on her great work.

From Maine to Florida, from Canada to California, thousands of her daughters sing the praises of the humble servant of God who fought so valiantly for her faith, whose sanctity earned for her the title of "the greatest single influence for good in her beloved land, America."

On the door of St. Patrick's Cathedral in New York City there is a beautiful bronze relief of Mother Seton entitled "Daughter of America." She is indeed a daughter of America, and the hope of America as well. The first steps toward her canonization have been taken, and Americans pray that one day Betty Bayley Seton may be known as St. Elizabeth of New York, first American-born saint.

Mother Seton's "Dear Remembrances" was found, and is preserved, practically in its entirety.

Catherine (Kitty) became a Sister of Mercy, Mother Catherine Seton. She lived to the age of ninety.

Richard died at sea at the age of twenty-five, saving the life of a minister.

William married, and one of his children became the Most Reverend Robert Seton, Archbishop of Heliopolis, who died at St. Elizabeth's Motherhouse, Convent Station, New Jersey.

Guy Carlton Bayley became a doctor and married Grace Roosevelt. Their son, James Roosevelt Bayley, became a Catholic, took Holy Orders, and eventually became the first Bishop of Newark, New Jersey. Later he became Archbishop of Baltimore.

Sister Elizabeth Boyle became Mother Elizabeth, first superior of the Sisters of Charity of Mount St. Vincent.

The daughter of the *Reverend Henry Hobart* entered the Catholic Church with her husband in 1854.

The Seton home at 8 State Street is now the Church of Our Lady of the Rosary serving 10,000 parishioners.